FOURTEEN

There is much laughter,
a few tears, and a lot of growing up
when you're

FOURTEEN

MARGIE RAY

THE STORY OF A WONDERFUL YEAR

Review and Herald Publishing Association
Washington, D.C.

Editor: Bobbie Jane Van Dolson
Cover Illustration: Lou Skidmore

Library of Congress Catalog No. 80-13365
ISBN 0-8280-0011-5
Printed in U.S.A.

For Fay, Richard, and George

CONTENTS

FOURTEEN

Those who read this book in the prime of adolescence will no doubt understand and be able to identify with much of it. But for those of you who are past the tinseled years of teen-agerdom, go back, if you will, and relive with me all the glory, the giddiness, the turmoil, of adolescence and the search for answers to life's questions, and the desire to be complete in this thing we call love.

PULLING UP ROOTS

IT was a hot day in August when the conference van loaded up the furniture and our boxes of belongings and carried them far away to the town of Willow Run. It really wasn't a great distance, but it seemed as far as the moon to me, who was soon to be leaving my friends and the surroundings that had been my home for four years. My sister, Maria, had graduated from the nearby Seventh-day Adventist college in Mansfield and had accepted a call to teach in a small two-room Seventh-day Adventist church school. So mother, Maria, and I were moving.

My brothers, Nicholas and Jesse, were living with our father, as things hadn't worked out for all of us to be together as a family. For this I was sad, but there was nothing I could do about it except go on living. And that's what I had done. Thinking about our split-up family always brought tears to my eyes, so as far as possible I had pushed it from my mind. It had been eight years since my father left and three since my brothers had gone to join him, and by this time I had gotten pretty good at repressing my unhappy memories.

So the van came and went, leaving us with only the barest necessities for living. Mother and Maria had to finish up their jobs at the sanitarium and college before we could leave for our new home, where we must get settled before the fall school term began. The days passed, but never without my wondering what it would be like where we were going and what the kids would be like at the new school, and whether I would fit in and be accepted by the others, who would already have their own friends.

But nobody knew that I had any fears for the future. I could keep up such a good front that people never knew I had problems unless I decided to tell them. I liked giving everyone the impression that I had a lot of confidence in myself, and I wasn't about to destroy that image. Mother and Maria had no doubts that I would fit in with the kids in the new school, but still I

wondered, and I hesitated to express my own doubts concerning
it. Finally I concluded that, since I had broken into a new group
once before, I could do it again—I'd have to. And so the days
passed, and with them my fourteenth birthday.

One day mother and I went shopping for a fall wardrobe to
begin the new school year, for most of my clothes were becoming
too short or worn. We carefully selected an armful of dresses off
the rack and proceeded to the dressing room. First, I tried on a
red-brown one decorated with an appliqued apple that had a
worm in it. To my delight, it fit. Quickly I tried on several of the
others and came finally to the cute blue-and-yellow plaid with
the dickey. My mother, busily hanging the other dresses back on
their hangers, happened to mention that "some people wear them
without the dickey" just as I was pulling it over my head. My
mouth dropped open and I exclaimed in horror, "Well, I would
never wear it that way!" Mother hadn't noticed that the dickey to
that particular dress came down very far in the front. Shocked by
my tone, she glanced up in time to see the reason and the look of
horror on my face, and burst into laughter.

"Well, what's so funny?" I asked.

Mother was still chuckling. "Usually, dear, the dickeys
aren't so low-cut," she replied. I was beginning to see the humor
in the matter, and the more we thought about it, the harder we
laughed, until the tears were rolling down our cheeks. Finally we
managed to get the dickey in place and decided that it was a very
nice dress after all.

With the new dresses bought we moved along to the shoe
store, where we purchased loafers for me. Last of all I bought
some underthings.

My mother and I had always been close, but the past year or
so had been stormy for us both. It seemed to me that she just
didn't understand me anymore and that my ideas about growing
up were a far cry from hers. She was always talking about things
I needed to improve—my hair, my room, my homework. She
always seemed so angry when she approached me about these that
I had a habit of tuning her out. And, needless to say, this didn't

add to the peacefulness around our home.

It seemed that she always tried to make me feel guilty for my indifference over the above-mentioned areas. Besides this, I resented it when she sided with Maria. Whenever there was any friction between the two of us Maria, who was seven years older and practically a straight-A student, was always right and I was wrong.

Through it all, however, never once did I doubt that they loved me dearly—perhaps that is why I felt I could always say what I thought to my mother and sister. Daily evidence from the past fourteen years had convinced me that I could talk freely to them.

Before our move we had made a visit to the principal's house in Willow Run, and I met the Dunlap family. As we drove up in front of their home a cute little brown-and-white dog, which I thought must be but a puppy, barked and ran the length of the chain-link fence. Later I found out he was nine years old and his name was Elliot. Mr. Dunlap was gone that day, but his wife greeted us pleasantly. Mrs. Dunlap was a very down-to-earth woman with a sense of humor. She would be the typing teacher and teach an English class for the fifth- and sixth-graders and home economics for the eighth-graders. They had a daughter, Jeannie, who was a year older than I and a grade ahead. She was friendly and easy to talk to. Then there was Aaron, a lively 5-year-old with a crew cut.

I hoped that Jeannie and I would be close friends. I didn't know any of the other girls who would be in the classroom, and I felt a sense of belonging with her, since her father and my sister would be the teachers at the school.

As we talked, I learned that a girl was coming to live with the Dunlaps during the week so she could attend school. A boy named Gregory would also live with them. Gregory didn't worry me, but the girl, Kim, seemed like a threat to my having Jeannie all to myself as a friend. I didn't even like her name. But that was the way things were going to be. What could I do about it? There was much to ponder on the way home.

The thing I regretted the most about leaving Mansfield was parting with my friends, particularly Andrea Tucker and Laura Wilson, lovingly termed Willy. We three had become fast friends at school. It was kind of funny. When we were paired off in twos we were the best of friends, but we could never seem to get along together when we made up a trio.

Now nights were spent at one another's houses for the last time. One last Monopoly game was played in bed with the covers near at hand to hide the evidence when my mother came on the scene to hush the laughter and turn out the light for the third time. Vows were made to write long letters and to stick by our friendships—no matter what—and the half-dreaded, half-longed-for day of departure arrived.

Two friends of Maria's—Louise and Margaret—helped us move the last of our belongings in a small U-Haul trailer. On the turnpike we kept passing a big Mack truck, which, in turn, kept passing us. After a while we figured that enough was enough, and sped down the pike and out of sight.

Fifteen or twenty minutes passed uneventfully, and then we heard a truck approaching from the rear with its horn beeping repeatedly. Glancing in the rear-view mirror, Louise informed us it was the same one. The five of us ignored the truck and the two fellows in it with team cooperation and wouldn't so much as turn our heads to glance at them.

Pulling off the turnpike at Willow Run, we came to a red light. But that persistent truck followed us, beeping all the while. Finally unable to restrain any longer, I turned in my seat and stole a glance at the two fellows in the Mack. Imagine my surprise when I saw one of them frantically waving my mother's lampshade at us while both of them roared with laughter. Then it was our turn to laugh. Needless to say, we pulled over to the side of the road, leaped out of the car, and retrieved the lampshade. It seems that the canvas covering our possessions in the trailer had blown loose some miles back. The men had seen the lampshade make its exit and had stopped their big rig to fetch it. Then came the mad chase and their desperate attempts

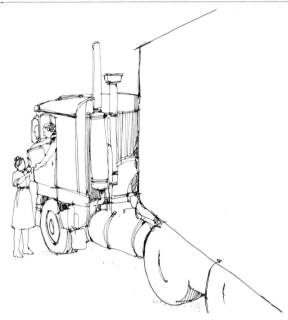

to get our attention. How we giggled as they helped us secure the canvas with some hanger wire. With many thanks and more laughs we were all on our way.

The remaining daylight was filled with unloading the U-Haul, returning it, making last-minute arrangements, and having supper.

Since we couldn't afford twenty dollars or so for a motel to house the five of us for the night, we decided to take our chances sleeping in the trailer house that would be our new home. It was still sitting on the back of the sales lot.

Getting into the trailer was a job in itself, as all sixty-five of our previously delivered boxes were practically wall to wall in the living room and higher than most of us in height. We conquered the task with the aid of one small flashlight and decided to go right to bed. With no electricity, what else was there to do? The next problem was safety. Since the trailer was not yet leveled, the doors would not close. But Maria brought in the ropes we had used with the U-Haul, and we tied them shut as best we could by flashlight and piled boxes against them in the hope of a safe night—without uninvited visitors.

We rose early the next morning and went to a restaurant to clean up a bit and have some breakfast. That day the men from the sales lot moved our new home into the park of our choice, Red Lick Run. I got to ride in the cab that pulled the trailer to the park. What a racket it made! The bird's-eye view I had from up inside the cab was a real switch from Louise's Dodge.

Mother and I got busy arranging and organizing our things, and Maria busied herself in getting ready for the big plunge, her first teaching job. At last our diligent work paid off. We were settled and cozy, and life in Willow Run had begun.

READY,
GET SET . . .

AFTER getting moved in, there was time for playing with my chipmunk, which had accompanied us all the way from our old home, and for exploring the woods and the land round about Red Lick Run.

The trailer park was situated on a main highway, but behind it stretched country roads, one of which followed a railroad track into Willow Run proper and to the church school. How I enjoyed hopping on my bike and riding anywhere my heart desired! It was neat to find out where the roads went. There was almost no traffic, and pedaling my bike gave me a chance to be alone with my thoughts while the early-morning and late-afternoon sunshine warmed my shoulders as I rode. I missed my friends terribly and looked forward to their newsy letters, which arrived less and less frequently as time went on. There didn't seem to be any kids my age, though I had made the acquaintance of a number of dogs. I still missed my own dog, Moochie, so much. We had had to get rid of him the last time we moved, three years before.

Riding down the road that led out of the park the back way, I came to where the road jogged over the railroad track. There I made a right turn and kept on going past several farms and what appeared to be an old castle-type estate.

"How I'd love to live in a castle," I said aloud to myself and to anything else that might happen to be listening, "and ride horses instead of bikes. I'd have my bedroom in the top of one of the spires, with a rope ladder descending to the garden below, and I'd sneak out and ride off in the night with my Prince Charming." Who knows where my fantasies might have taken me had I not hit a bump in the road? This brought my thoughts back to where I actually was and made me realize that I was again nearing an intersection. Making another right turn I followed the road out to the main highway and took one more right turn, which led me to the front entrance of Red Lick Run. It was a refreshing ride, several miles long, and one that I took often after that, either alone on my bicycle or on foot with my mother. Hereafter I shall refer to this route as Jason's Square.

It was a happy event when my dad and brothers, Nicky and Jesse, brought Maria a car to drive. It wasn't the newest one going, but it ran fine and we were grateful and excited at the prospect of owning some wheels. Gas was considerably cheaper back in the mid-sixties, and we would often go out for a joy ride on the country roads. Some miles distant we found an old general store that had the most delicious ice cream. It was fun to explore the unknown.

Our first Sabbath morning in Willow Run arrived bright and clear. The three of us dressed and got ready for church. I didn't feel much like eating—I got a knot in my stomach every time I thought of having to face all those people for the first time. But I had to do it. So in my red jacket dress that had a potted flower appliqued on it, and with my Bible in hand, I climbed into the car for the five-mile drive. Services were held in the school gymnasium, and we found a number of cars already there when we arrived. The knot in my middle grew tighter as we got out and went toward the building, where a group of small children were laughing and talking on the porch. Then came the introductions. I managed to smile through them all and even said a word or two now and then! At least I looked confident even if I didn't feel that way. Besides, the people seemed very friendly.

At last it was time to go inside for Sabbath school. I felt self-conscious and awkward as we walked to an empty row by the side door from the hallway. It was the third or fourth row from the front, and I thought, Well, good. At least I'll have my back to nearly everyone and won't have to look at people unless those in front turn around to gawk. They did.

Up front, the piano on the right of the platform was sending out quiet music. Streams of sunlight shone down in angles from the high windows of the gym. I recognized the pianist as Mrs. Dunlap. If I could have known the good times I would have in that very gym I would have felt very comfortable, but I couldn't, so I just sat there nervously and waited for things to begin.

There was a class for the youth in the back, and at the urgings of Maria I found my way to it for the lesson study. I would just as soon have spent the time out in the car or roaming the fields—anything to avoid the uncomfortable. A very friendly man named Adam Jenkins taught the youth class, and I liked him at once. He had such a warm smile and welcomed me to the class as if he really meant it. The lesson was on men from the Old Testament, and the young people answered the questions. It was a good feeling to be there, after all. I spied Jeannie Dunlap and she flashed me a friendly smile, which reinforced the good feelings.

After the Sabbath school lesson I somehow found myself next to a large woman, and she too, seemed pleasant. I felt very shy about sharing the songbook with her. I thought I really should be careful whom I made friends with, as I didn't want to be too closely associated with a minority group right off the bat. The fact that Trudy (as I later learned was her name) was heavy classified her as a minority to me. But since it was the polite thing to do, I did share the book with her and we sang the closing song together.

During church I sat with my mother and Maria. In front and behind us everywhere were families with children of all ages. Every once in a while, when opportunity permitted, I stole a glance around at the people across the aisle and behind me. Each daring attempt was returned with a stare-down from some equally curious and bolder onlooker. I would immediately cringe and look straight ahead once again. The minister, Elder Spencer, gave a good sermon. Afterward there was more milling around in the foyer and more introductions. During church we had noticed a lonely-looking soldier in uniform, probably from the nearby Army base, Fort Douglas. My mother thought it would be a nice gesture to ask him home to dinner and to spend the rest of the Sabbath day away from the barracks. Wayne gratefully accepted the invitation, and it turned out to be the beginning of an interesting relationship. Since he was Maria's age he came often to see her, and sometimes the fun times included me—such as long drives to the northern part of the State, and to New York City, or trips to Chinese restaurants.

On Sunday morning Maria and I went to the little school and helped paint the classroom in which Maria would be teaching. I had used a roller brush only once before, but the paint went on easily and the immediate results proved to be very satisfying.

When I was taking some trash out I met a boy with a crew cut and wrinkly gray pants that were too short. I remembered him as the boy who had sat with the family in front of us in church the day before. It was his mother with whom I had shared the songbook. He was friendly enough, and we soon found out a few things about each other. His name was Ryan Branson and most people called him Ryder. He would be in the ninth grade, the same as I. He had gone to school in Willow Run since first grade and acted very knowledgeable about the place in general, although he did act somewhat shy to me. But the merry twinkle in his brown eyes left me with the impression that fun times were ahead.

ON YOUR MARK . . . GO!

THE old familiar knot returned to my stomach on Wednesday morning as I got ready for school. (Monday there had been more cleanups, and Tuesday was dedicated to registering for the school term.) Only this morning the knot was double and tied a little tighter than usual. I slipped into one of my new dresses, combed my hair, and ate as best I could in the excitement of it all. Maria and I arrived at school early, as she still had last-minute preparations to make before the children arrived. I had time to be concerned about several things. What kind of a teacher will Mr. Dunlap be? How will I do scholastically in a small school? In grade school I had been only an average student, except in spelling, home economics, and reading. I had felt inferior to the kids who earned better grades than I did, and, of course, I always felt lower than the kids who had undivided homes with both parents Seventh-day Adventist Christians. What I wouldn't have given for that kind of family. Now I wondered how I would fare in this new school and what the kids would be like.

The students began to arrive singly and in small groups. First came a black girl and her two younger sisters. Her name was Karen Maxwell and she was to be in ninth grade also. Karen had a sense of humor that was obvious right from the start, and when she laughed her deep brown eyes joined in. She was tall and wore her hair short. Mrs. Maxwell had a job at a nearby silk mill, and she brought her girls to school early in order to get to work on time. They came all the way from Burbank, a good half hour's drive.

Next Elder Spencer drove up and dropped off his boy, Edgar. Edgar looked a lot like his father and was very neatly dressed. Lisa Jenkins arrived with her two younger brothers. Lisa was very thin and had brown hair about medium length. She would be in eighth grade, and her father was the pleasant man who had taught the youth Sabbath school class. Then another black girl arrived—Nettie Blossom. She also had a younger brother and sister. Since it was nearing time to begin, the students began to file into the classrooms.

Another eighth-grader, Katharine Herman, came with her two younger sisters. It seemed that everyone, except Edgar and me, had younger siblings.

And then Jeannie came around the corner of the school with Kim and Gregory. Gregory wore tight white pants and had longish blond hair. He was teasing Kim, who was dressed in a red plaid skirt with a red tailored blouse, knee socks, and desert boots. Both were stockily built. Kim had a pleasant face and seemed nice enough.

As I said before, I wasn't any too eager to meet Kim, but as all things come about, I met her. In fact, she sat right in back of me and Jeannie sat across the aisle from her—diagonal to me. Finally Ryan arrived, completing the classroom that Mr. Dunlap taught. There were ten of us in all, ranging from grades eight to ten only, since there were no seventh-graders that year.

Mr. Dunlap's large wooden desk was up front on the left-hand side. Windows ran the length of the room on that side and plants rested on their sills. Green chalkboards covered the walls on the right and front of the room. Behind the chalkboards in the front was a coat room with a board shelf where we kept our lunches and brass hooks below to hang our wraps in cold weather. At the back of the room was a black marble-top counter with a sink. We would make use of this during science class.

In the back, on the side by the windows, was a door that led into a small library furnished with one long table and several chairs. Shelves of books covered one entire wall. A door led out the other side near the main entrance of the building. And there was a small picture window between the classroom and the library. White venetian blinds hung on the window, and these could be opened and closed at the touch of a string.

The ninth- and tenth-graders sat at two rows of desks by the windows. Each desk opened from the top, and its accompanying chair was connected by a metal bar extending from under the seat down to the floor and up again to the under part of the desk. In the first row the seat nearest the front was empty. Behind it sat Karen Maxwell, Jeannie Dunlap, and Gregory Connors. In the second row in the front was Edgar Spencer, then my desk across from Karen's. Kim Wink was third, and Ryder Branson sat in the back seat across from Gregory. On the other half of the room by the blackboards and in the back by the main door, where the pencil sharpener hung, were the eighth-graders:

I was shocked when Mr. Dunlap asked one of the students to have opening prayer. Imagine having to pray out loud in front of the whole class! The student took the request very nonchalantly, as did the four others who were asked that day. I quickly figured out that if there were five prayers offered each day and only ten pupils, that would mean each would pray at least once every other day. I was sure, however, that Mr. Dunlap sensed my petrified state, because he went all that first week without once asking me to offer a prayer. I felt certain it was coming, though, and I listened carefully so I would have some idea of what to say when the time came. I had gone to a large Seventh-day Adventist grade school the four years previous to this, and there were thirty-one students in my eighth-grade class. The teacher had prayed most of the time or else asked for volunteers. Of course, I never volunteered.

At recess we played volleyball in the gym. The platform for the church services remained there throughout the week, but the piano, the pulpit, and the folding chairs were removed.

Volleyball was something I wasn't very good at, nor liked, but that was the only game going, and everyone else seemed to enjoy it, so I took my place and made a mighty effort to do what the others did. But try as I might, I could *not* get the ball over the net. It was very humiliating.

Back in the classroom we had algebra class, and Mr. Dunlap gave us an assignment that floored me right from the start. It seemed as though he gave a big assignment in everything. There had been two lessons in Bible and a whole chapter to be covered in our English workbooks.

After algebra class I filed nervously into the typing room with the rest of the ninth- and tenth-graders. The entrance to the typing room was to the left of the platform in the gymnasium. What would learning to type be like? Mrs. Dunlap assigned each student a typewriter to use, with the exception of Karen, who brought her own manual Olivetti. I sat staring at the machine in front of me as Mrs. Dunlap explained that we would be given a short time to learn the keyboard, then the figures would be covered over with small circles of green tape and we would have to rely on our memories. We spent the first period getting acquainted with our individual typewriters and doing a simple exercise. Then the bell rang and it was time for lunch. The students chattered with one another and had a merry time of it. Greg did seem like a bully. He was always teasing that poor Kim girl.

I had learned that Kim was a fairly new Adventist, having been baptized only the December before. Her folks were separated and she lived with her mother and grandparents. I felt a little sorry for Kim, with Greg always teasing her so much, but she seemed to take it in stride. I decided to make an effort to be nice to her, since she was new too, and a "new Adventist" besides. That would be the polite thing to do. Little did I realize at the time the dividends I would reap from that decision.

Gradually I began spending more time with Kim. Two of the things that attracted me were the fact that she had a sense of humor and that she used big words, some already in existence, and some that she invented on the spur of the moment. One day when Greg was teasing her again (yet?) she looked at him and spouted off: "How dare you insinuate that I should tolerate such a indiabolical situation, you insignificant piece of psychological ingenuity!"

One of my early impressions of Gregory was that he was a whiz in algebra because he got a 100 percent on the first paper. But later he seemed to make about as many errors as the rest of us.

After lunch we had a study period while Mr. Dunlap taught the eighth-graders their Bible class. Then came world history. If there was one thing I hated, it was history, and world history was the worst. The book was so boring. Who cared how civilization got started around the Mediterranean anyway? The class period seemed to drag on for ever so long. Recess was like a breath of air to the faint. It seemed that there weren't many who enjoyed history class.

Then we had a practice period for improving typing skills, followed by one more study period while the eighth-graders were taught science, and finally the closing song, "Turn Your Eyes Upon Jesus," and prayer. At 3:15 school was over for the day.

I worked on my assignments while I waited for Maria. In the car on the way home we talked about the day. Maria had fifteen pupils in grades one to six and sounded excited and hopeful. It had been a good day and I looked forward to spending many more. The kids seemed to like me and I liked them. So far, so good.

And so the days passed quickly, all structured in the same basic pattern, but each with different incidents and happenings that always seemed to make today a little better than yesterday. As for public prayer, my luck didn't hold for long. On the following Monday Mr. Dunlap asked me to offer prayer *twice* on the same day. Both times I offered up a short one and to the point. When I said "Amen" nothing happened. I was a little surprised, but then I didn't really know what I had expected would happen. Oh, well, maybe it wasn't going to be so bad after all.

Greg had two older sisters who had attended the same academy that Maria and my brother Nicky had gone to. He and I had vague recollections of seeing each other on visits to the school, so there seemed to be a tie there between the past and the present for the two of us.

Kim, Karen, and I began spending more and more time talking and laughing together. It was such fun and the days began to move in rapid succession.

About this time somehow, from somewhere, Greg picked up the notion that Chevies (and General Motors products in general) were better than Fords. Of course Kim and I disagreed. This friendly argument lasted through the whole year. I don't think there was a Ford or a Chevy that went by the window that wasn't noticed and remarked about. Nor was there a lunch period that this same matter wasn't discussed. What a time we had of it!

Just a week after school began Maria fell prey to some type of "bug" that was going around. She fainted in the bathroom and was put to bed for several days. During this time there was no one to substitute and so I volunteered.

"I'll teach for you, Sis."

She lay there a moment considering. Her first response wasn't negative; rather it was more neutral and even leaning a little toward the positive. So I decided to help swing the pendulum a little more in that direction.

"I could do it. Just help me with the lesson plans for the material you want covered. Mrs. Dunlap's too busy with her own schedule. I'm sure I could do it," I repeated for the third time. "My work can be caught up easily enough," I confirmed, glowing with enthusiasm.

"Yes, I don't doubt that you can. Dial the phone for me, will you? I'll ask Mr. Dunlap."

Mr. Dunlap's consent sent me into a dither. Just think of it! Happily I faced the challenge of handling her fifteen pupils in grades one to six, not to mention the elation I felt when I thought of lawfully missing my own classes.

The next day Trudy, Ryder's mother, came to pick me up, and I went in before Maria's class as confident as could be. I could do it; I knew I could, and I was eager to get this show on the road.

I called the roll, had morning worship, and began handing out assignments to keep the rest of the classes busy while I soared into one Bible lesson after another. What was that Mr. Dunlap had said the day before—"Idleness is the devil's workshop"? Well, we would have none of that in *my* classroom. After several

reading circles, it was time for recess. I was enjoying myself to the full. The only problem I had was one of the fourth-graders. After putting up with about half a day of smart talk, I called him to my desk and informed him that he would report to Mr. Dunlap's office, at the principal's earliest convenience. Things went a little more smoothly after that, as the first- and second-graders began to realize that perhaps being "smart" doesn't always pay. When the disturbance ceased, it was easier to concentrate on the lesson material. And except for a dirty look from the boy now and then, we got along all right after that.

I enjoyed the math classes (algebra should be so easy!) and also geography and science. The day was so filled with one activity after another, that the time passed amazingly fast. Mr. Dunlap dropped in now and then to make sure I was all right. It really was a satisfying experience.

Two days passed much the same, and finally Maria was feeling up to taking over her charges once again and I returned to the ninth-grade class. It was good to be back, even to the tauntings of "school marm" and "Miss Montgomery" from my peers.

NAMES WILL NEVER HURT ME

ONE morning early in the school year, Mr. Dunlap tossed the keys to Greg, who proceeded to go to the office, where he and Edgar undertook the task of carting out the school scale and bringing it to the classroom. Then Mr. Dunlap began his twice-yearly ritual of measuring the students. Everyone's height and weight were recorded in his little grade book for later reference. My height at the time was 4 feet 10 inches and I weighed but 89 pounds. Skinny and little and proud as a peacock would probably best describe my condition. Kim weighed 140 pounds (a real fatty in my book) and was about 5 feet 4 inches tall. Greg was slightly heavier and just a hair taller than Kim. This was the beginning of a new argument between the two of them as to who was indeed the larger and also led to all kinds of suppositions as to what the final measuring in June would reveal.

We must have loved friendly arguments, for they figured in nearly everything we did. Another such one got started over the rather strange subject of the Irish and the Welsh, and which was indeed superior. Now the question was settled in my mind. Having Irish blood coursing through my veins was all the evidence I needed. But Kim, who claimed to have a wee bit of Welsh in her, was a hard one to convince. Oh, how we loved to tease! Kim's Welsh grandfather's name was Louis Llewellyn, and my Irish grandfather was Francis Gallagher. Every time a hint of praise for one nationality would emerge, we would seize it and capitalize on it to the handicap of the other. Every song service turned to a race to see who could have their Irish or Welsh tunes sung first. My favorite was "I Know Whom I Have Believed," by James McGranahan. And Kim's was "Guide Me, O Thou Great Jehovah," an old Welsh hymn. They were, by the way, right across the page from each other in the songbooks we used that year. And so the bickering continued back and forth for the rest of the term (and indeed for several years after that), all good naturedly, of course. One thing led to another, and soon we had sayings like "If Old Lady Llewellyn hadn't thrown Helen in the watermelon, it would have been very good for sellin'." And Kim's great toe on her right foot would be set into a thumping action—something that happened whenever she was upset, angry, or trying to think of a good counter reaction to the Irish, Chevies, et cetera. We called it her Welsh toe and teased her about it whenever we caught it in motion unawares to her. Her right sneaker even had a hole in the top of it from all of the vigorous workouts that toe received—something that amused us all.

As the days moved by, we five ninth-graders spent our afternoon typing sessions in the room alone. It was during this time that Mr. Dunlap taught the two tenth-graders, Jeannie and Greg, their general business class. Perhaps it would be accurate to say that we were getting acquainted with one another more than with our typing. And it wasn't long before others began making snide little remarks (all in fun, of course) about Ryder and me, all of which I strongly denied but secretly enjoyed. Indeed, the same thing was happening to Kim and Greg. The students seemed to come and go in the afternoon typing session, and it seemed more often than not that Ryan and I found ourselves alone. On one such occasion I asked him about some typing example, and he came up to read it and discuss it. Suddenly, as he was leaning over the book, he looked up with his arm still around the back of my chair, and said, "You know how everyone's been teasing us?" I nodded and he went on. "Well, I think if we just ignored their comments they would soon quit bothering us."

By the way he said it, I knew that he liked me, and I felt the same way about him. I wished he would kiss me, but he didn't. He seemed uneasy, almost as if he were afraid. I laughed to myself, but said nothing.

So from that day on we took the comments without denying them. A few days later Ryan came to class with a last year's school picture for me. I accepted it and tucked it into a corner of my desk where I could look at it often. His hair had been longer then, and with his dark eyes he did seem handsome indeed. I took the picture home that night and carefully tucked it in my box of treasures.

I had never taken an interest in keeping my things neat and in order until Ryan's picture came to stay. Almost every evening I tidied up that green box before I went to bed, whether it needed it or not. Then I began getting fussy about the drawer I kept it in. After that was set in order my growing mania for good housekeeping spread until my drawers and even the top of the dresser were kept immaculate. Finally my half of the closet and even the bed demonstrated the result of my new frenzy for neatness.

Maria, shocked at my turning over such a bright new leaf, marveled much but said little. It was no longer a fight to get me to make my half of the double bed we shared. And Fridays were a little less frantic, since the bedroom was already neat for the approaching Sabbath day.

And the same energetic and ongoing tidiness carried over into the classroom. My desk got the past-due cleaning out that it so desperately needed and deserved, and it continued to remain in an orderly state.

After several weeks this fever of organization began to become a part of me. Mr. Dunlap said that when you do something fifteen times it becomes a habit, and gradually I came to dislike any slovenly appearance. Ryan's desk was no exception. Several times I commented on the rat's nest he was harboring. He just laughed at this, though it seemed to bother him a little.

I was about to give up in despair on his desk situation, when to my surprise one day he called me back to have a gander at his "rat's nest." I was absolutely shocked: it was clean! It had taken nearly two hours, and he had filled the waste-paper basket, which he had borrowed from its normal corner, twice, but he accomplished his goal.

"What a difference!" I declared. "You deserve the seal of good housekeeping!" He could tell I was pleased, and he beamed like a first-grader whose drawing had just been praised by the teacher.

While we are on the subject of Ryan's desk I might add that nearly every morning he would open his desk top and help himself to part of the contents of his lunch bag. How he thought he was escaping notice I have yet to figure out. Perhaps that's why he chose one of the back seats at the beginning of the term. Without fail, during algebra or study period up would go the desk top and the smell of an orange or cake or whatever he decided to devour would waft out to tantalize the rest of us. We giggled over his display of starvation. We never learned why Mr. Dunlap let this continue. Maybe he felt sorry for Ryan's being hungry or perhaps the aromas never quite made it that far.

Though nearly everyone else called him Ryder—a carry-over from childhood—I preferred Ryan and began calling him that. The class seemed to be pretty close, each enjoying the others' company.

One day at recess after one of my poorer volleyball serves, Lisa made the comment, "Boy, you're worse than I am." That set me to thinking, and very determinedly I resolved that small as I was, I would get that ball across the net or die trying. With a little practice and much determined effort I finally managed to serve the ball properly. And when I could do it right, I discovered that volleyball wasn't such a bad sport after all. In my great efforts I had acquired the name Mighty Mouse. My brother Nicky, who was also small, had carried that same name in academy, so I was proud to carry it too. And now I felt that I really belonged.

Kim's last name was Wink, and so, with a mouse on the team, it was very fitting to carry over her nickname from public school—Kim Wink the rat fink. One thing led to another, and before we knew it we also had a Karen the Heron and Juvenile Double Delinquent in our midst (Jeannie's initials were JDD).

One day during the lunch hour we were carrying on with the usual jokes and exchange of unimportant information.

"Hey, Kim," taunted Greg, "I know one time you'll have to

ride in a GM car. You'll just have to."

"When's that?"

"They make hearses!"

"Well, over my dead body," Kim declared, and then added as if in exasperation, "These Chevies and GM products are going to drive me to the grave yet." We all cracked up.

Then Ryan sounded off with, "Say, do you know what F-O-R-D stands for?" And without waiting for a reply he went on, "*Fix Or Repair Daily.*"

Somehow the topic turned to middle names. Now, I have no particular dislike for my middle name, but for some reason that day I decided not to disclose that piece of information. Everyone soon knew everyone else's middle name.

"What's yours, Marcie?" asked Greg.

"I don't have one," I replied, with a laugh that plainly told them I was teasing.

"Oh yes, you do," said Ryan.

"Will you tell it if we guess it?"

"Maybe."

"Just tell us what it begins with."

I would not until they finally guessed "T."

"Timothy," guessed Ryan.

"I bet it's Midget," said Greg.

"No, that doesn't begin with a T," Ryan reminded him.

"Oh, well, then, Tidget," Greg corrected himself.

Somehow that name stuck and was used interchangeably with Mighty Mouse, even after I finally told them that my real middle name was Theresa.

One day while Kim, Karen, and I were working on algebra together in the library, we figured out the problems with relative ease. We were so pleased with our accomplishment and so giddy that day that we decided we could do with a few distinguished titles. So just for fun we sat there at the table choosing up names appropriate to the occasion. It was finally settled that we should be called Marcie the Magnificent, Karen the Great, and Kim the Wonderful. Our abdominal muscles got a good workout over that one. Later on in typing, I was relating the incident to Ryan, who felt a little left out, not having a title of his own.

"Have no fear," I informed him. "We have one picked out for you."

"What's that?" he asked eagerly, his face brightening.

"Ryan the Rodent," I flatly replied. Just then the bell rang and I hurried to the classroom.

THE MONOPOLY FRIENDSHIP

ONE afternoon during typing practice class we got off on a strange tangent. Several of us wondered aloud about Mr. Dunlap's age. We did a survey on how old everyone thought him to be, and the answers ranged from 39 to 63. In order to find out who was the nearest to being correct we would have to obtain the pertinent information. The problem was how?

Finally it was resolved that we would ask Mr. Dunlap during algebra class how old he was when he got married and then ask Mrs. Dunlap during typing class how long they had been married. We figured that if we asked them both in the same morning, they wouldn't have time to confer and figure out our angle until after we had the data we sought.

Well, the plan worked fine. During recess the next day we rehearsed our tactics once again. In algebra we "inadvertently" got into a discussion about the proper age for marriage. After some debate, Mr. Dunlap gave us the reply which we had been subtly seeking during the entire conversation. He had been married at 23 years of age. Algebra class ended, we mosied into the typing room with confidence born of one victory in the conquest of our goal.

Mrs. Dunlap, being the pleasant-natured person that she was, made it very easy to approach her regarding the matter. We simply asked directly just how long she had been married. Her reply was sweet but not so short. She not only informed us that they had been married 23 years, she proceeded to launch into many irrelevant but interesting details. After class we deductively figured out that Mr. Dunlap was 46 and his wife 43. (She had also informed our eager ears that she was three years younger than he.) After putting our bits of information together, we felt smugly satisfied.

It had been decided that Mrs. Dunlap would give me piano lessons on Tuesday afternoons. So each Tuesday I would walk home with Kim, Jeannie, and Gregory for a lesson. And instead of my walking back to the school, Maria picked me up at Dunlaps' whenever she was ready to leave.

It was during one of these visits that Kim and I learned of another similar interest, that of playing Monopoly. We struck up a friendly game of it, which we failed to finish before Maria came. We decided to finish later and carefully put rubber bands around the money and deeds each owned, marked our places on the board, and put the set away. The game continued on Tuesday afternoons for three weeks. When it was finished, we began another. We played numerous games, each lasting several weeks, and every time we played, Kim lost. No matter if she was banker, deeder, both, or neither, she couldn't seem to win.

There was one thing she succeeded in, however, and that was just about breaking my neck in the frequently scheduled pillow fights we had during the games. It's a wonder we never broke anything in all our scuffling about. After we tired of throwing pillows, we would sit back down and make an effort to resume our play.

It was over those games that we were able to talk freely and honestly express our feelings and thoughts on many subjects. The Monopoly game set the climate for speaking what was on our hearts, and we grew to appreciate each other and the problems we faced. And so the friendship grew.

One Friday afternoon I visited Kim and found that Greg had been up to his old teasing tricks again. This time it was watermelon in her hair. So Kim washed her hair for Sabbath, and while it was drying we resumed our game.

Kim rolled the dice and landed on Atlantic.

"That will be twenty-two dollars," I reminded her.

"Just subtract it from what you owe."

"In that case I only owe you four dollars, so you have four to the good. Such luck you have."

I rolled the dice and landed on Boardwalk, which Kim owned.

"That's fifty dollars." I got change for a hundred from the

bank and paid the debt, totaling fifty-four dollars. Whenever we owed each other less than fifty dollars, we would just figure it out mentally, saying we either had so much "to the good" or "to the bad" whichever the case might be. When one of us accumulated a debt of fifty dollars or more, we would go through the rigmarole of evening things up.

"Now we're even-Stephen," I commented. Just to be out of the ordinary we would pronounce if "Stef-fan" instead of "Stephen." Indeed we said it so often that it sounded right to us, and whenever someone else used the expression even-Stephen, to us it sounded funny.

"Go ahead, it's your turn."

"You know, I've been trying to think of something I can do to get even with Greg for the watermelon bath he gave me," mused Kim as she gave the dice a mighty tumble and sprawled them on the board, knocking my marker from the "Just Visiting" section into the jail.

"So what did you have in mind?" I put my marker back into place.

"Well, why don't we put a glass of water on his door, so when he walks in he'll get his head wet?"

"Good idea." We got a plastic glass from the kitchen and proceeded to the basement, where Greg's room was. On the way through the laundry room, we decided that soap powder might make things a little more inconvenient for him. So we filled up the glass and carefully balanced it on the top of the door, leaving the door slightly ajar as we departed.

"That'll fix him," Kim smirked with a note of triumph in her voice. We could hardly contain ourselves until Greg got home. Guilt feelings sometimes make one suspicious of the actions of others, and Greg was no exception in this case. He figured, and well he might, that he would be repaid for his latest misdemeanor, and so with utmost caution he opened the door to his room, peering about cautiously for something out of the ordinary. The door had been swung open so gently that the glass of detergent remained undisturbed, and Greg had failed to catch a glimpse of it with his wandering eye. He continued to check over the place for salt in his bed, short sheets, and whatever else he could think of that might be used as a practical joke.

Meanwhile, back at the Monopoly game, Kim and I were dying of curiosity. We had expected that he'd come storming upstairs eager for revenge, and his delay aroused our curiosity. Then we surmised that he might take care of the mess and act as if nothing had happened. In order to avoid that we rushed downstairs. Kim went flying into the room first to have a good laugh at Greg, jarring the door in the process and thus causing a sudden downpour of detergent on her newly washed hair! I couldn't suppress the laughter, nor could Kim for that matter, and Greg thought it was the most hilarious thing he'd ever seen.

THE CHURCH SOCIAL

I WAS nicely settled in the school routine and enjoying every minute of it. The only thing that troubled me was guilt feelings that I experienced from time to time about things I had done when I lived in Mansfield. If I could have talked to someone about it, it might have been a great relief to the hollow aching inside, but there was that proud, self-confident image to retain in other people's minds. These were things I couldn't even discuss with my mother. Many times I weighed the matter in the balances of my values, but every time the scales tipped to the same side. No, I would bear it alone inside and maintain the image no matter how badly my heart hurt sometimes. Often I had prayed about it, and I knew God had forgiven my sinful conduct, but I just could not seem to shake off the overshadowing cloak of guilt that settled down heavily upon me.

The only thing I knew to do was pray that God would keep me determined to build a better reputation in Willow Run, and then perhaps someday these feelings would cease and I could see myself as a different person.

I really did want to do what was right. But sometimes it seemed that all my efforts were in vain. I'd been baptized at 12 and somehow expected that the baptism itself would make a difference in my behavior. But before very long I found myself living almost the same way I had before. I had not yet learned that victory cannot come from one's self. And the devil was right there to inform me that my conversion was not genuine—that I was a sinner and always would be.

It was nearing the middle of fall and the days were growing cooler. A jacket was a necessity whenever one went outdoors. The pale sunshine felt good as it shone through the window of the car on our way to church on Sabbath morning.

In the youth Sabbath school class I happened to sit next to

Ryan's older brother, Kenny. During the lesson I glanced down at his Sabbath school lesson quarterly, which was open on his lap. In black ink and with his boyish handwriting he had neatly written in the answers to the questions. Sitting there I got to thinking about Kenny. He seemed gentle and intelligent and a real Christian. He was older than I and attended the academy upstate at Jerome. Now he was home on leave for the weekend. My thoughts continued. Other people studied their Sabbath school lessons too; I surveyed the class and it seemed that the ones who did were easy to pick out by their speech and deportment. Inspired by the correlation I saw that day between lesson study and exemplary life styles, I decided that I, too, would begin studying.

From that time the Sabbath school class came alive to me. The more I studied, the more I could take part and the more meaningful the Bible became to me. It added a new dimension to my life.

In the afternoon a group of us young people and a few of the leaders in the church banded together and drove to several places that housed older folks. We brought some "sunshine" to them with singing and prayer and by talking with them. I particularly enjoyed the opportunity to get together with the kids from the church who didn't attend the church school.

Betty, Lisa's older sister, was always there, along with Rosie Denver and several others. Another of my favorites was Scott Kaiser. His folks lived right across from the school. They were a very large family, and the parents couldn't see their way clear to give any of the children a Christian education, so they all attended public school. I wanted to get better acquainted with Scott, but his quiet way made it difficult for me, as I could be shy at times too.

We had sunshine bands often, and when we weren't out singing we would hand out literature, to help the folks in the surrounding area learn a little more about Adventists in general and the Willow Run group in particular.

On the Saturday night of Thanksgiving weekend there was a

church social at the gym. These gatherings were the most fun times. Only one thing was lacking, or perhaps I should say two things were missing. Kim and Greg always went home to Windsor for the weekends. I missed them, but usually the students from the academy were home, adding to the liveliness of things. This particular night there were marches accompanied by toe-tapping music. It seemed that everyone took part. Many of the church families were there. Now that I knew them, I realized that a large number of them had real handicaps—broken homes, retarded children, cripples, health problems, members of the families who were not Adventists, et cetera, but the overall picture they created was one of happiness that is borne within the heart when the Lord comes to stay. Kenny Branson was in high spirits that night and we had lots of fun. During the evening, Trudy gave me some pointers on volleyball that helped increase my skill, and I appreciated her interest.

While cookies and punch were being devoured some of the adults played table games in Maria's classroom, and we who made up the younger set were left to our own devices. Several of us sauntered down to one end of the hall and sat talking. The only lighting was the reflection from the brightly lighted gymnasium—thus giving a darkened effect that we didn't mind a bit.

Finally Lisa and Betty left for home, and then some of the others drifted off to practice volleyball and such. Finding ourselves alone, Ryan and I launched into a conversation all our own. It was neat to be together and so close. His brown eyes danced even in the shadowy dimness. Very nonchalantly he positioned his foot alongside mine on the chair. I took this to be quite an honor. It's funny how such little things make an impression on young lovers and stay so vividly in the memory. We laughed and joked quite a while, and I took the liberty of playing with the buckle on his boot.

We heard someone at the water fountain and glanced up to see Doug Lexington peering around the corner at us with a suspicious scowl on his face, but he said nothing. A few minutes later my mother appeared at the drinking fountain and looked around the corner at us with an expression of curiosity.

Her only words were, "What are you two doing down there?" To which we replied, "Just talking."

"Well, why don't you come up and talk in the gym," she added with an I'm-not-asking-you-I'm-telling-you tone in her voice. And with that she returned to the table-game room.

Disgusted, we reluctantly obeyed her desire.

"Oh, *mothers!*" I voiced, a bit emphatically.

Ryan just laughed and guided me into the gym. I liked it when he did that. We surely did have fun. It didn't seem to matter what we were doing as long as we did it together. Several times we slipped back into the darkened kitchenette area behind the door on the right of the platform and continued our private conversation. I was ecstatic and did so hate to see the evening end.

When we got home it was late, and as I was preparing for bed I heard my mother calling me to her room, where she was already bedded down for the night amid roller net and bed covers. I stood there waiting to hear what she had to say. Mentally I voiced the thought, Here we go with lecture No. 72.

"What were you two doing down that hall tonight?"

"I *told* you, just talking," I replied irritated.

"What did you have to pick *that* spot for?"

"I don't know—because we wanted to, I guess."

"Well, it certainly didn't look good."

"Looks aren't everything," I replied, holding my breath after I had said it, for fear of causing World War III.

"Well, I wasn't the only one who was concerned—Doug Lexington was too, and so were some others."

"Like who?"

"Never mind." I felt she sometimes used expressions like that for added emphasis in the point she was trying to get across. That avenue closed, I pursued another.

"Well, what did Doug tell you?" I asked in a tone of voice that implied that I doubted that whatever he said was true.

"He said he didn't know what was going on down there, but

it didn't look too good."

"Oh, *brother!*"

"Don't act smart," mother said ominously, raising up on her elbow a little farther. "I'd better not hear of anything going on—ever!" She shook her finger for greater emphasis. "After all, you've got your sister's reputation at stake."

I knew it was futile to argue further. But my mind raced on—"my sister's reputation"— How do you like that? So hers is more important than mine now!

"You won't," I said and walked back to my room. I refused to let her dampen my spirits. I had had a wonderful time and she wasn't going to spoil it. Reliving my favorite parts of the evening, I climbed into bed and drifted off to pleasant dreams.

INGATHERING ESCAPADES

AS the weather continued to grow colder and winter approached, Ingathering season arrived. Kim and I could hardly wait for the first night. Kim, being newly baptized, had not as yet participated in the church's annual fund-raising campaign. But I assured her that there was lots of fun to be had and we wouldn't let a minute of it escape us.

At the school that first evening we divided into groups, and each little band piled into a car and traveled to an assigned section of the town. Arriving at our area, which happened to be a middle-class development, Kim and I rehearsed the minispeech once more.

"I'll talk at the first couple of houses until you get the hang of it," I said.

While we were walking up the first driveway Kim nervously whipped out a jawbreaker for each of us. "Here, have some battery acid, as Mr. Dunlap calls them," she offered. And as we approached the first door each of us had a small mobile lump on one side of our cheeks.

For some unknown reason every time we got into a situation where there was tension Kim and I would begin laughing over every little thing. Well, that last comment about the battery acid set us off for the evening. We were giggling by the time we knocked at the door. When the lady of the house answered, the laughing increased until neither of us was able to say anything. Things went from bad to worse, until one of us finally was able to blurt out, "Just a minute."

Fortunately the woman was young and very understanding and just joined in our merriment until I was able to tell her the purpose of our visit. To our surprise she gave us a contribution. Then when we left her house we laughed from embarrassment. And so the hilarity perpetuated itself. Despite it all, we came in with a tidy sum of money.

The students were encouraged to Ingather, and homework was excused for those who did, so nearly all of us participated. Every night Kim and I went door to door together. On Friday night Kim's mother came to get her as usual for the weekend. Saturday night Kim went Ingathering with the Windsor church members and I went again with the Willow Run group.

One night Lisa's sister, Betty, and I went together. On the first street, only women answered the doors at the first nine houses. Before knocking on the tenth door we peered through the window and saw a man standing at an ironing board with an apron tied around his waist.

When he came to the door I began what had become that night's habitual greeting, "Good evening, ma'am. We're out this evening . . ." Well, the strain was too much for Betty, who burst out with a great peal of laughter. Then to my horror I realized what I'd said and was immediately overcome by loud guffaws.

Oh, I questioned to myself, I wonder if he thinks I called him that because he had an apron on and was ironing when we

came. How embarrassing! Finally I managed to get my voice back and tried to explain things. The man was very understanding, much to my relief, and took it good-naturedly. His wife was in the hospital with their new baby, and he was trying to manage things at home.

Kim was back Sunday night and we went out together again. Even though I had solicited before, Kim always seemed to bring in more money. She attributed it to the beanie cap she wore on her head each time she went out, much to Mr. Dunlap's dismay.

This particular evening, tired of all the bulky coins we were receiving and the lack of the more portable dollar bills, we decided to try another approach, using the line "We're out on our annual dollar night collecting funds for . . ." To our astonishment it worked.

As we proceeded down the street we took turns soliciting. At one house when it was my turn a woman opened the door and I began my spiel about our annual dollar night. Asking us to wait a minute she ran and fetched a dollar bill, but put it in Kim's can. We thanked her, and when the door was closed behind us, I demanded that Kim turn the money over to me, who had solicited it.

"OK, Old Lady Llewellyn, fork it over."

"Fork what over?" As if she didn't know what I was talking about.

"My dollar bill, that's what."

"*Your* dollar bill?"

"Yes, *mine,*" I said with emphasis.

"Tsk, tsk. Remember what your sister says: possession is nine tenths of the law. Besides, she gave it to *me!*"

"Look here, you flat-footed rat fink, if you won't give it to me, I'll take it. Thank you." And so saying I reached over and snatched the dollar bill from her can, where she had a profusion of them on display. That is, I snatched half of the dollar bill—the other half must have seen things Kim's way, for it decided to remain. At least that was her explanation when it came time to count the money later that evening. Needless to say, we had a hard time knocking on doors after that. Well, actually it wasn't the knocking so much as the trying to talk without giggling.

The next week things took a turn for the worse. We ended up in Mr. Oglethorpe's car. Now, Mr. Oglethorpe was a very stern type—all business. Indeed the only redeeming quality that we girls saw in him was that he drove a Ford. Upon arriving at the territory for the evening he let it be known that he expected each of us to take one side of the street and solicit separately. His manner was so gruff and matter-of-fact that neither Kim nor I had the nerve to say anything. Mr. Oglethorpe was not the type of person you argued with.

Solemnly we got out of the car and headed into the darkness with our collection cans and pamphlets explaining the work the previous donations had helped to accomplish. It had snowed earlier, leaving a thick white blanket on the ground. Kim and I decided between ourselves who would take which side and began knocking on doors. Mr. Oglethorpe took the other four solicitors to different sections of the area to be covered that night. We two worked steadily and, arriving at the end of the block, started down the adjoining street. Mr. Oglethorpe drove past slowly, checking on us once, and then disappeared.

When we came to the next street we decided to continue on around the block. Things were dull until it came to deciding who should take which side. Since Mr. Oglethorpe wasn't in sight, one of us yelled, "First come, first served." And with that we both dashed to the side with the fewer steps leading up to the homes. Trying to crowd each other out of the way we collided and lost our balance while scrambling over a mound of snow. Kim hit the pavement with a thud, and I was sprawled out on the walk. My skirt flew up in the tussle and all the part of me it normally covered became frosted over with snow.

In the crash my money can overturned, spilling its contents over the sidewalk and down into the snow. Accustomed to taking most misfortunes good-naturedly, the two of us sat there shaking with laughter and thankful for the darkness to cover up our foolish Ingathering shenanigans.

"It's a good thing Brother Oglethorpe didn't see *that!*" Kim exclaimed.

Just then the lights of a car parked about twenty feet away flashed on, spotlighting both of us still in our crash-landing positions. Startled, we glanced up, the merriment on our faces vanishing as we recognized the car as the one in which we had come, knowing only too well that behind those blinding head-lights Brother Oglethorpe's smaller but no less accusing eyes were upon us.

Mortified by his unseen presence we quickly got to our feet, gathering up our pamphlets and stray coins in the process. Suddenly the other side of the street seemed like a welcome refuge, and we both rushed in that direction. Finally I turned back to take the previously fought-over side. When the territory was completed we faced Mr. Oglethorpe, cringing at the thought of the lecture we would receive. We were thankful to be the first ones in the car, so the others would not witness our reprimand-ing. Embarrassed though we were for our behavior, we each shot an understanding look at the other and laughed inwardly. Brother Oglethorpe sternly vowed that we would not be allowed to Ingather together after that escapade.

"What a hag!" I whispered to Kim at the earliest opportu-nity.

We talked it over between ourselves and decided that we would rather go out twice as many times and be together than go out separately only half as many times. Hereafter, we vowed in turn, we would avoid Mr. Oglethorpe's car like the plague.

BOYS AND
GOALS

INGATHERING busied our out-of-school hours and made the days seem to have wings. Reminiscing in the weeks that followed, Kim and I admitted that we particularly enjoyed going when we rode in the same car as Ryan and Greg. At such times we quite naturally paired off, Kim with Greg, and I with Ryan, whenever possible. What was that feeling that I felt in my breast—that delicious excitement—every time I got around that boy? I wondered if Kim felt the same about Greg.

Many an afternoon, flung over Kim's bed, we discussed Greg and Ryan and our future prospects. Jokingly we would (between ourselves only, of course) refer to their respective parents as "my mother-in-law," or "your father-in-law," et cetera. However, the fellows weren't by any means the ideals of what we thought we would settle down with when we got married. Dreamily we talked of how we would change them to fit the ideal pattern of the Prince Charming we expected to marry. (How much we had to learn!) This remarkable transformation would come in time, we reasoned, and for the moment we were enjoying the roles we played in their lives just then. After all, weren't they two of the most admired kids in the school? There were various reasons for this popularity, but that mattered not an iota to us. We had our own reasons for liking them and enjoying their company. For us they were satisfying the adolescent urge for companionship with the opposite sex, and we liked to think that the feelings were mutual.

So it was with considerable consternation that Kim observed Greg's interest in one of the eighth-graders, Katharine Herman.

Volleyball was beginning to take a back seat by now and we were enjoying a number of other forms of recreation. On rainy days we loitered around the gym, roller-skating or playing whatever game struck our fancy. We particularly liked "Wink'em." Half of the students would sit in a circle of chairs and the other half, plus one extra, would stand behind them. Whoever was extra would have an empty chair and would wink at a person sitting down in hopes that he or she would be able to escape to the vacant seat. The people behind the chairs had to stand with their heads bowed, looking at the back of whoever occupied the seat in front of them. And their hands must remain at their sides. Whenever someone winked at a "captive," the person behind the summoned one must quickly tag a shoulder before he/she got away. The game was great fun.

Kim particularly enjoyed stealing Greg from Katharine's chair, and I always liked having Ryan respond so readily to my wink.

Some days I couldn't figure out whether Ryan really liked me or not. I was afflicted with a very bad case of the "likes" for him, but he seemed to be fickle at times. I put up with it for a while, and then I sought out a chance for revenge.

One particular rainy lunch-hour recess Ryan seemed to delight in winking at all the other girls as much as, or more than, he did at me. So when it came time to switch and the girls did the winking while the boys did the moving around from chair to chair, I saw my chance.

I winked at Greg and Edgar a couple times each and also at a girl or two. (Since we had three boys and seven girls, the girls had to be boys now and then!) By the time I got around to winking at Ryan he was eager to hop over to my vacant chair. When he turned around to sit down in it, thankful for the chance of getting away without being tagged on the shoulder by his captor, I quickly moved the chair back a foot or so, and he landed on the floor. The look on his face and the laughter of every one else made me feel quite revenged.

Back in the classroom things improved. Funny how things like that help to balance themselves out, I thought to myself. It was beginning to be a pattern—one that I would find true many times over in my relationships.

Mr. Dunlap usually let us choose books from the library and read them for a period after lunch. We loved it and thought we were "getting away with murder," being able to read for a whole period every day. It seemed too good to be true. Little did we realize that we were storing up a treasure of knowledge gathered from the wholesome books we were poring over with such fascination. It opened up a whole new world to us. Mr. Dunlap knew all this but said nothing, letting us read on with the impression that we were getting away with something. We read book after book, many of which were biographies. The thrilling fulfillment of the lives in the stories made us long for such adventures as unfolded on the pages.

"Wouldn't it be neat to be missionaries?" Kim asked me one day.

"Oh, yes, that would be so cool!"

"I'd love to be a teacher and teach in a mission school somewhere."

"I'd rather be a nurse."

"Wouldn't it be cool to work together?"

"Yeah, and maybe marry guys who wanted to do the same thing?"

Our enthusiasm was growing.

"I'd like to marry a minister."

"And I a doctor," I said.

"Let's do it."

And so it was decided that we would become a teacher and a nurse. Kim would marry a minister and I a doctor. And that was that.

It seemed that our decision was the beginning of the fulfillment of a song we had sung together when we had unknowingly attended the same kindergarten Sabbath school years before:

> We are a missionary band,
> Missionary band,
> Missionary band,
> We are a missionary band,
> Doing all we can.

THE MISCHIEF-MAKERS

WE really weren't *bad* kids. But I think the combination of our unique personalities didn't help the mischief situation at all. At the beginning, being new and shy, I tended to lean on Jeannie's example for support. Since her father was our principal and teacher, she always seemed to try to be a model student and ease his burdens. It took me a full nine weeks to realize that I couldn't be anybody but myself. I had tried in my own little way to be a carbon copy of Jeannie, thinking that maybe it was the proper thing to do since my sister was also a teacher. That, coupled with the uncertainty as to what kind of grades I would make, kept me subdued for a while.

I'll never forget the morning at the end of the first nine-week grading period when Mr. Dunlap called us all into the library individually to discuss our scholastic progress and his impressions of us in general.

Solemnly I walked toward the library when my turn came. My palms were sweaty, and the old familiar knot tightened in my middle. But I hummed as I advanced, hoping that the self-confident attitude that people expected of me would come to my rescue.

Closing the door, Mr. Dunlap lost no time in getting to the point. He commented favorably about my school work in general. And much to my astonishment he concluded with these words:

"Your presence has been a real asset to our school, and we're pleased to have your good example."

I thanked him, because it seemed the proper thing to do at the time, and walked back to the classroom. I have never been able to figure out what brought about the sudden change in me. Perhaps it was because I felt a surge of welcome relief that my grades were good (I had received all B's except one, one that was an A) or perhaps the fact that Mr. Dunlap had indicated his approval of me, made me a bit giddy, or something. Anyway, the fact is that from that time I seemed to lose the inhibitions I had felt about mischievous behavior.

Kim was next in line. As I approached my desk I spied a tack on the seat. Aha, I reflected, no one is going to trick me into sitting on that. Glancing around the room I saw that Ryan had signed out. (Whenever we wanted to use the bathroom or get a drink we had to sign our initials on the chalkboard nearest the back door. Only one person at a time was allowed to go out.) I lost no time in snatching up the tack and "replanting" it on Ryan's chair. A moment later I was working with ardent effort in my English workbook when Ryan returned to the room. As I had hoped, he "got the point" at once, then made his way up to my desk and laughingly inquired if I had sat on it. He didn't seem terribly disappointed that I hadn't.

In the meantime Kim's session was over and Jeannie was called back. Then in half horror and half-excited delight I watched as Ryan walked purposefully to the front of the room and placed that tack on Mr. Dunlap's chair.

The rest of the class waited with bated breath for the outcome of the situation. Of course everyone was working earnestly on his English workbooks when the last teacher-student session was finished. Nobody signed out for fear of missing the staged drama's outcome.

Mr. Dunlap made his way to the front, his mind no doubt occupied with the previous hour's events. He lowered himself into his chair and hence onto the tack, but gave no indication of the painful puncture he must have received. He simply went through the customary routine of clearing his throat and conveniently removed the tack as he reached for the handkerchief that always occupied his back pocket when not called upon for active duty.

Of course we were disappointed in his response, but there was nothing to do but continue with our studies. We even wondered if he had missed it somehow, though it hardly seemed possible, since his large frame occupied every inch of the chair.

We weren't long in wondering, however, as another series of individual conferences began in the library. Needless to say, this round wasn't as pleasant as the first had been.

I was determined, however, that I was not going to miss what could be perhaps the only opportunity to find out if the joke had been effective.

After reluctantly answering the questions he fired at me, I seized upon the opportunity.

"Did it hurt?" I inquired.

"Well, let's just say I felt it," he replied. Then as if to change the subject he moved on into the implications of a puncture wound—lockjaw, et cetera.

Finally I was released from the question-and-lecture session and returned to my seat. But the barrier was removed, and the way was opened for many future pranks.

A similar incident with a very different outcome happened one day when Edgar decided to place half of a peeled orange on Kim's seat. How anyone could overlook something the size and color of an orange I have yet to figure out. But overlook it she did; and Kim, with her stocky frame, was not noted for delicate landings.

Returning from some errand she flounced into the chair in her usual manner. But the results were unusually spectacular. Of course, Kim was never one for letting a sleeping dog lie and was up in two seconds flat. With the orange still clinging tenaciously to her skirt, she headed for the grave offender.

Edgar made rapidly for the rear door. As Kim rounded the last seat in the row she was right behind him, and decided to just even up things properly by giving him a good kick. She might have been successful in settling the score, had Ryan been able to subdue this sudden impulse to grab her foot in midair and give it a yank. And if Kim thought she had squeezed out all the juice from the fruit that still dangled from the skirt, she had a surprise. That second landing extracted even the seeds from the mangled remains of Edgar's orange, as well as screams of laughter from the rest of the students.

In typing practice Kim and Karen and Edgar often finished their exercises before Ryan and I did, and we two would remain in the room alone. On these occasions Ryan often slipped over to the door and locked it. It was so neat to be alone with Ryan even for just a little while where we could talk undisturbed. And I knew the feeling was mutual.

But after a few minutes we would hear footsteps approaching, and the jangle of Mr. Dunlap's keys would warn us that we'd better get back to work. And more than once, while our teacher was searching for the right key to unlock the door, Ryan would scurry over and open it quickly, saying innocently, "Oh, I was just leaving."

It is doubtful that this little act fooled Mr. Dunlap, but it gave us a little satisfaction. And it was even more gratifying to be able to give a juicy report to the ones back in the room who were dying to know what had happened.

GROWING PAINS

OUR plans to become missionaries seemed to help Kim and me to have a clearer idea of the changes we hoped to see take place in Ryan and Greg. We at last had some concrete basis to picture in our minds' eyes. We prayed that God would fulfill our plans.

And God heard our prayers and set about to answer them in the way that would give us the happiest fulfillment, but we had to be patient as the future unfolded in His good time.

Our plans for mission service gave us a new direction in life. We had a goal to work toward, one that would help shape us into the kinds of young women God could use.

We had both made plans for the future before, but now these were put aside and forgotten. Our new plans seemed of a greater magnitude—of real lasting value that would stand the test of time.

We began going to prayer meeting. After the discussion period these were always closed with a season of prayer. Anyone who wished or felt impressed to do so could pray at that time. Public prayer was easy for Kim, and her example inspired me to want to profess God openly by praying aloud before a group also, but I was scared to death.

During one particular meeting I was in a sweat just thinking about praying. I wanted to so badly, but the inhibited side of me strongly opposed any such notion.

I sat there getting warmer by the minute. I realized time was running out and if I was going to pray that evening I would have to make a firm decision to do so or else wait until the following week. I tried to decide what was so scary about it and concluded that I was afraid that I wouldn't be able to remember what to say once I got started. So I decided to make up a list of several things to pray about and use the list for reference if necessary. I jotted down several things. Then I poked Kim in the side and showed her my list to get her approval, since she seemed to me to be such a "pro" in this matter. She seemed a bit surprised, but glanced at my prayer list.

"Is there anything else I should add?" I whispered.

"Yeah, that you can read your writing."

That nearly changed my mind about praying that night, but gradually I took heart again, and by the time the prayer part came I felt that I could do it. I waited for a chance to get my "widow's mite" of a prayer in edgewise.

I began in Kim's habitual manner of "Dear heavenly Father . . ." only to be drowned out by another, much louder, voice using the exact same words. I nearly lost all nerve over that and surely hoped no one had heard my feeble attempt.

When all was quiet I started again, using the more familiar approach of "Dear Jesus" and this time got the floor with success. I was probably the only one that night who prayed with her eyes open, but I had to see what I had written.

Sweat was pouring off me by the time I finished, but I felt so good about everything afterward. It was worth all the agonizing effort, I felt.

Kim and I walked back to Dunlap's, where Maria would pick me up after she was through doing some last-minute things in the classroom after the meeting. We walked slowly discussing what was on our hearts. We wanted to be good. Jeannie was good, but she seemed too good. We even felt she was a little fanatical sometimes. Finally we concluded that we would be good but not fanatical, whatever that meant.

Sundays often meant some pleasant activity with Wayne, the soldier stationed at Fort Douglas. He could show Maria and me the best time. He was always cooking up some interesting thing for us to do and some unusual place for us to go. One day he took us on base to explore the old tanks that had been used during World War II. I was delighted. Army stories had always fascinated me. He also took us down to the rifle range that day, and we met Claude, a huge St. Bernard dog owned by one of the officers. Another time Wayne gave me a picture of a chipmunk that he had blown up to 8-by-10-inch size. He had waited on a log 45 minutes for the animal to come out of its hole. And many were the times when this obliging fellow would race to our house from the base to catch *my* chipmunk that had escaped. It was he who taught Maria how to drive. And once he took us up north to an optometrist friend of his and had our eyes checked and new glasses made.

Wayne would wrestle with me and talk with me. He showed me how to play some songs on the piano. He was good to me and I loved him for it. It was like having Nicky or Jesse in the flesh again—a big brother relationship that was so important to me right then. Wayne always seemed to understand the need I had to be silly and to be myself. He was quite a card himself.

Three times that year he asked Maria to marry him. Unfortunately for Wayne she didn't feel the same about him, but she did enjoy his friendship.

I thought it was so romantic when we rode in the car and Wayne and Maria sang songs like "Smile Awhile" and "Ah, Sweet Mystery of Life." How I wished it were me with *my* Prince Charming.

And many were the times when I would be "asleep" on his lap while Maria was getting in some driving experience. At these times I would hear all sorts of interesting tidbits about their feelings for each other, et cetera. Sometimes they even talked about me, at which time my ears were particularly attentive.

One sleepy Sunday morning, Maria's voice interrupted my daydreams.

"If you don't hurry up, you're not going to be ready when Wayne comes in twenty minutes."

Twenty minutes! Oh dear. I would have to hurry. I donned comfortable clothes and hurriedly gobbled some morsels of toast and cereal followed by an orange juice chaser. This particular day he was taking us to the World's Fair in New York City, and I was in great glee.

He arrived precisely on time, as was his custom, and we left. It was quite a long drive, and we sang a lot on the way. There were many things to talk about, too. Finally, we arrived in the parking lot. I don't think I've ever seen so many cars. A vast ocean of autos stretched as far as we could see.

Once inside the gate, we found ourselves standing in long lines waiting to get into the exhibits. It was a great practice in patience. But nearly every one was worth the wait. The day sped by, and it was late when we finally left the fair. We stopped at a restaurant for something to eat, but I was so tired from the day's activities that I fell asleep before the food was served. Being a sound sleeper, I didn't know another thing until I woke up about eleven the next morning. It had been a glorious day.

When I arrived at school on Tuesday Ryan asked me if I was feeling better.

"I wasn't sick," I informed him.

"I know. Your sister said you were exalted from the fair."

"Don't you mean exhausted?" I inquired.

He was so cute at times. His shy boyishness was shining through and I liked it.

CHRISTMAS AND TOGETHERNESS

THE coming Christmas season caught us in its bustle, crowding out serious thoughts of being "good." Nearly everything we did was accompanied by the munching of ribbon candy that Kim's grandmother had sent back with her.

At recess time we filled the minutes with sledding and snowball fights. Across from the church school was a vacant lot, and on beyond that was a wooded area with several nice runways to sled down. Even after school we would make our way over there and wing down the slopes time after time, with snow-ballings and face washings in between. We would pile up four and five high on the sleds and have a grand time.

Since I was the smallest I usually occupied the top of the pile. This gave me the advantage of not being squashed by the others but the disadvantage of being thrown from the sled whenever we hit a bump. Nevertheless we enjoyed every minute of the adventures. Only a select few of us took part in these sledding occasions after school. Lisa, Greg, Ryan, Kim and I made up the group. Jeannie usually had something to do at home, and the other students either had to meet parents or catch rides. Katharine Herman was one of these, to our relief. It seemed that she was being a bit over-possessive of Greg these days and even showed a somewhat decided dislike for me. Several times I wondered if she was jealous of me—but then I could never figure out any reason why she would be, so I just shrugged it off.

Afternoons after school we could enjoy Greg's company, and he seemed freer in his actions with us then. It was almost a delight to take a spill in the snow, knowing that "our guys," as we considered them, would be there to lend us a helping hand and then carry the sleds to the top.

In school we were busy getting ready for the Christmas program that we were to give for the parents and the church members. Mr. Dunlap had decided that we would present a play on Abraham Lincoln. Tediously we worked to memorize our parts and make the costumes. Hours were spent in the gym in devoted practice.

One day, in the late afternoon, we were restless and not very dedicated to the task of preparing for the program. Mr. Dunlap, who was tired of prodding us and getting nowhere, was also at the end of his rope. We had only one more rehearsal and things were not going smoothly.

Over and over again we went through the three stanzas of "Joyful, Joyful, We Adore Thee," and it seemed as if we got more mixed up every time. Finally the dismissal bell rang, and in his frustration Mr. Dunlap ordered everyone who couldn't say the words by memory to stay until they were learned. Needless to say, Jeannie alone was excepted, and the other nine of us remained. We made a motley-looking crew. Weary of the strain of a long day, the thought that we were still not allowed to leave was almost too much to bear.

But somehow we managed to commit those lines to memory and be excused.

"What a taskmaster!" we mumbled.

Things went better the next day, and Mr. Dunlap was encouraged that things might turn out all right after all. Last-minute details were ironed out to his satisfaction, and the backdrop for the play was in place.

"Be here sharply at 6:30 P.M.," were his last words of warning.

We arrived backstage in good time and began dressing for the grand finale. Jeannie, who was to be Abraham Lincoln, got into her dark presidential-looking (we hoped) clothes that we had raided from the Dorcas room upstairs and her tall stovepipe hat made from construction paper. Faces were blackened appropriately for the slaves, and makeshift costumes donned. Mr. Dunlap was tense as he gave us last-minute instructions and warnings to be on our best behavior.

In the bustle no one noticed Ryan making his way to the kitchenette behind the door on the right of the gym, where

Kim's clarinet sat waiting for her solo later on in the program.

We were getting hot from all the stage clothes when Mr. Dunlap finally gave the cue to begin. Obediently the performers took their places on the stage and began acting out the skit. As I marched out in my soldier-type band-uniform outfit I could hear Wayne and Maria cracking up in the audience.

Everything was going all right until Greg stood before Jeannie, who was flushed and sweltering in the heavy presidential garb in which she was clad. The stovepipe hat was inching its way down farther on her forehead. In an attempt to move it back up a little without very obviously correcting it with her hands, she began a rapid succession of eyebrow-raising exercises.

Under the nervous tension of the moment Greg interpreted the twitching eyebrows as something humorous and began laughing. The more he laughed, the more his mind was distracted, until finally he could no longer remember his part. And then he laughed from embarrassment, as did some of the rest of us. Mrs. Dunlap was trying to prompt him in the background, but he couldn't hear her whisper because of the snickers. Finally Jeannie whispered his next line for him and he was able to finish. Mr. Dunlap sat rigidly on the front row, a look of consternation on his face.

The play out of the way, we got on with the rest of the program. My part was a poem that went fairly well. It was followed by a few other selections, and then Kim reached for her clarinet and strode to the music stand. She licked the reed to moisten it as Jeannie played the introduction on the piano. Kim was very good on the clarinet and projected a nice tone quality.

The song she had chosen, "What Child Is This," began on a sweet note, and the melody flowed forth beautifully until about the end of the second line, when a loud squeak jerked us all to attention. Kim calmly continued playing until she came to the same note in another line. Again the clarinet squeaked unmercifully. Kim proceeded doggedly. When she got to the last line the same B-flat note repeated itself several times over, squeaking plaintively with each attempt. And so it continued with each stanza. After the solo Kim returned to her seat in a very mortified state. We were all shocked by such a flop. I wondered what had happened to Kim's capabilities. But the mystery was solved when Ryan informed me that he had stuck a piece of paper under the B-flat key, thus causing a squeak to issue forth each time it was pressed. Upon hearing what had happened, Kim had mixed emotions, none of them pleasant. She felt relief that the fiasco was no reflection on her abilities, frustrated to realize that the audience *didn't* know that, and absolutely furious at the culprit.

"Wait till I get my hands on him!" she croaked out in a whispered rage.

Who knows what personal revenge she would have taken had not Mr. Dunlap collared him first?

With the program ended, our Christmas vacation began. It was painful to be separated from Kim for ten days, but I was delighted that at least one of my big brothers could be there for Christmas. Nicholas arrived on Friday evening. Most people called him Nick, but I got away with calling him Nicky. He was six years older than I and always treated me with such gentle, brotherly love that when I thought about it during the long separations, I would cry. Why did he love me so much? And why did I love him so fiercely in return? I cannot help but think that God puts in our hearts the family ties that so strongly bind brothers and sisters. Even the years of separation couldn't seem to make a dent in the bond of love.

I eagerly scanned the pile of presents he placed under the tree. Tomorrow was both Sabbath and Christmas, so we would be waiting until after sundown before satisfying our curiosity as to the contents of the parcels. I could hardly wait.

With great joy I looked forward to Sabbath evening with Nicky there. Whenever we were all together there was such a good feeling of closeness. The conversations would range from individual problems to future plans and dreams and back to recollections of years gone by. But whatever the topic we always ended up on the subject of love. It was such a good feeling to be able to discuss things so freely. Lying awake in bed that night I relived bits and pieces of our time together and reexperienced the warmth that had surrounded us. I wished it could stay that way for always.

"Yes," I whispered to myself, "love will always be a part of our everyday conversations in my home. My children shall grow up with the right attitude toward love and everything else." And so with these pleasant thoughts, I drifted off to a peaceful slumber.

Seven-thirty came too early after going to bed so late, but once I remembered that Nicky had spent the night, I was up and dressing in great haste. It was Christmas Day. Besides Nicky being there, all the kids would be home from the academy, including Ryan's brother Kenny. In anticipation my stomach coiled into its knot. This time, however, it was a happy knot, if you know what I mean. And, too, there was company coming for dinner.

Breakfast was a hurried affair, and before long we were all in Nick's '64 Ford speeding down the back roads to the church school. Nicky was the "Jehu" in the family, and his furious chariot driving this day was no exception. It didn't seem to matter to him when he missed the turn where the road jogged over the railroad track (part of Jason's Square) and we slid into a snowbank. It was all so sudden we didn't have time to be upset, and by the time we thought about it, we were backed up and going again, with no harm done. I just shook my head and said to myself, "Old Jehu's at it again. Dear Lord, please watch over us."

Church and Sabbath school were both fun. I particularly enjoyed song service. Nicky had requested "Under His Wings." I felt secure that day, as if I were under warm and protective feathers. Nicky, who had left the church when he and Jesse had gone to live with my dad, was coming back. It was probably unnoticed by most everyone else, but I was aware of the gradual softening as the Holy Spirit was working on his heart. He had willingly gone to church with us that day, and it was he who insisted that we postpone the opening of gifts until after Sabbath. He sang with such meaning in his voice that I could tell there was a growing relationship with Jesus. I was excited and thankful.

I sat there with my Sabbath school lesson quarterly with the filled-in answers. I would like to have spoken to Kenny and thanked him for his good influence, but I didn't. For one thing, Ryan was there with his red jacket on and looking extra handsome, which took up a great deal of my attention. It had been several days since we had seen each other, and we enjoyed catching up on small talk out in the halls between Sabbath school and church. Trudy, Ryan's mother, passed by and gave us an approving smile. It seemed she did that a lot lately, or was I just imagining? Feeling delighted and fulfilled, we went back in and sat down with our respective families.

It felt so good to go to church those days. I don't know why exactly. Surely it was more than just the excitement of the people there. I felt so secure and strengthened as a result. We went home to a delicious meal.

As the final dinner preparations were being made an old car pulled up out front. It was a '49 Mercury, a real heap. I had been playing watchdog at the window and saw it first. Before anyone could say or do anything, the car's operator had leaped out of the still-running car and shouted to us.

"Don't laugh. It's paid for!"

Good old Johnny; he hadn't changed a bit. He and Maria and Nicky had all been friends in academy together. We had the best time together that afternoon.

Saturday night was fun too. My dad had sent me a pair of ice skates and knee socks and mittens. I rejoiced, for now I could go skating at the pond. It was good to have evidence that dad still loved me. I saw him very seldom, and when I did he was the typical old-country type who demonstrated very little love to his children. Perhaps he thought we were getting too big for such nonsense. I was glad Nicky wasn't that way. My heart always warmed when I thought of my brother.

With the bustle of Christmas over, my long-standing wish for someone or something of my very own returned to me. I liked Ryan, it was true, and I was sure he liked me. I longed for him to take me in his arms and tell me that he did, so I would know for sure. All this guesswork discouraged me at times.

It was a Wednesday afternoon, late, when I approached the subject of going to the animal shelter and choosing a pet. To my great astonishment, both Maria and mother agreed. I had been waiting for months for this, and now it seemed too good to be true. We telephoned and learned that they would be open until eight. In great excitement and anticipation we drove to the shelter and I rushed in to the kennel area. There were dogs of every description. I wanted to hug and love them all, particularly the bigger ones. Finally I decided on a puppy that looked part shepherd and part boxer. I figured that if my mother wouldn't let me have one of the bigger dogs, I'd choose the pup with the biggest paws. Overjoyed with our purchase I gathered the lovable bundle in my arms and carried him to the car. It was a case of love at first sight for both the puppy and me. He was something of my very own! My mother suggested naming him Maverick, and the name stuck. Oh, what a comforting companion he would be in the weeks and months ahead!

Now my jaunts into the woods need not be alone. Maverick was at my heels the moment I said "Walk." And many were the times that I would pour out my heart's thoughts to him without any worries of their being passed on. Funny how thoughts and contemplated conversations always sound different—perhaps a little more dramatic—when you voice them. I would relive situations, except that this time around I would say things differently. And as for the shy moments with Ryan, well, I told Maverick exactly what I thought and confided my concern about how Ryan really felt about me. Who did that boy think he was anyway, keeping a girl in suspense? Maverick often whined sympathetically and committed himself to me with a wet kiss. He became, next to Kim, my best comfort in this world.

WINTER ACTIVITIES

AFTER Christmas, but while we were still on vacation, Johnny Baker came back for another visit, this time staying several nights. During the day, when mom was working at the diner and Maria was grading tests and marking report cards, Johnny and I had some long talks. I felt close to him, since the family had known him so long. We reminisced about the time he came home from academy with Maria and Nicky for Christmas. I recalled that they had mixed up a batch of Christmas cookies and put them in the oven, and while they were doing acrobatic stunts in the living room, the cookies burnt to a pitiful crisp.

Johnny could play the piano "by ear" better than anybody I'd ever known. You could just sing a tune once and the next time through he'd play it for you in any key you wanted. He was gifted, there was no doubt about it, and it intrigued me.

He and I shared an interest in big words. He taught me the word *bombastic,* and Kim and I immediately added it to our vocabulary. And he also got us started on the expression "Helen, please! I haven't had my 4 o'clock aspirin," which we also promptly adopted. What a riot he was! We did a lot of laughing while he was there.

By the time Christmas vacation ended, I was eager to get back to school. Not for the studies, mind you, but because I was so lonesome for the kids. And I felt pretty secure in the fact that the feelings were mutual. But if I thought my nerve would overcome my shyness and enable me to openly confront Ryan about his feelings, well, I was mistaken.

There was a sort of vibrant, electric atmosphere in the classroom that first morning, despite Mr. Dunlap's efforts to get things back to prevacation normality. After all, it had been ten days since we'd been together and there was a lot to catch up on. But finally, when Mr. Dunlap's stern side began to show through, we calmed down a bit. But where the whispering left off, the note passing began.

Somehow we made it through the morning, and, I suppose in an effort to relax us a bit, Mr. Dunlap read a story to us about Mabel, a heroine rather lacking in virtues. Mabel, it seemed, was grossly overweight (she enjoyed chocolate candy immensely) but was quite terrific in English. She had come from a fairly well-to-do family, and it was nothing for her to put a five-dollar bill in the offering plate on Sabbath. But Mabel, it seemed, never felt she got the attention she deserved. As the story continued, she began pretending to have fainting spells at the most inopportune times, much to the alarm of the other students and faculty members. The narrative proceeded, describing the struggle the rest of the characters went through to help Mabel face and solve her problems.

This was one time when Mr. Dunlap's psychology had reverse effects. Instead of helping us ease into the routine of school work, the story launched us into a lively discussion.

Kim, being somewhat overweight and excelling in English, immediately fit into the Mabel image—and that was enough to get our imaginations in gear. The telephone rang in the office and Mr. Dunlap went to answer it. The door was no sooner closed behind him than I turned in my seat to face Kim.

"Hey, Mabel, how about some help with this English assignment?"

"OK, for a box of chocolates."

"That's a deal."

"Psst." It was Ryan. "How about helping me, too?"

"Sure, I need the attention," replied Kim in mock sincerity.

"But you'll have to wait till we go to town for the chocolates."

"Well, I don't know if I can wait that long—I may faint by the wayside before then," she concluded in grave tones with raised eyebrows.

The bantering continued until we heard the doorknob turn. Then, of course, we became very studious. But the nickname

Mabel stuck with Kim for a long time.

By the next morning things were beginning to simmer down, and there was hope that we might actually learn something. That afternoon our trio, Karen the Great, Kim the Wonderful, and Marcie the Magnificent, made our way back to the library to tackle the algebra assignment.

Ryan sauntered back on a pretense of finding a book to read, and while he was there he closed the blind on the window that opened into the classroom. Mr. Dunlap nonchalantly reopened it as he passed through returning from a phone call. When Ryan found out that we girls were actually industriously working at the assignment, I suppose he figured that misery likes company and decided to join us. Four heads bent over the papers for an amazing length of time (considering the parties involved), with only brief interruptions now and then to seek help from Mr. Dunlap.

Whenever it was my turn to go up to the teacher's desk, I would snitch a leaf from one of Mr. Dunlap's plants. This particular one produced little granules that tasted sweet. I never did learn the name of it.

Ryan had again pulled the cord for the blinds to close, and Mr. Dunlap again very patiently reopened them, not mentioning the incident. By and by Kim and Karen had their fill of algebra and returned to the classroom to pursue other interests. But as I still had yesterday's assignment to catch up on I remained, and so did Ryan.

Greg and several others came in for books and then returned to their seats. The phone rang again and Mr. Dunlap hurried in to the office to answer it. When he reentered the classroom some time later, everyone was in his seat except Ryan and me—and the blinds were closed again. To make matters worse, Ryan had locked the door.

Mr. Dunlap said nothing, but in a few minutes he came back to tell us it was time for recess. Off to the gym for recreation we went, the recent battle of wits being the topic of discussion. Why did we derive so much satisfaction out of such things?

Soon, however, we were so involved in the volleyball game that everything else took a back seat. Ryan, who was stationed on the platform, attempted to return the ball over the net. Leaping into the air, he hit it with both hands simultaneously, fanning them out at arms length away from his body. In the process he projected himself a little farther forward than he had intended, and went into a perfect swan dive, landing directly on the floor below. It knocked the breath out of him and wounded his pride considerably, but he was otherwise unhurt.

We all watched with amusement. It was so funny. When I could finally bring myself to the point of talking again, I approached him regarding his spill.

"I'll say one thing for you, Ryder."

"What's that?"

"You were graceful." At that I broke up laughing again and fled, with Ryan in hot pursuit. It wasn't long before he caught me, and as I struggled to free myself he turned me around to face him, never letting go his hold. My first thought was, How romantic. It was pleasantly exciting to have his strong arms encircling me. He looked me right in the eyes—and his own were dark and flashing.

Is he going to kiss me? I wondered. Right here in front of these kids? If he did that now, they surely would be suspicious of all the time we spent in the typing room alone.

Just then Mr. Dunlap made his appearance at the door of the gym. He was the last person I wanted to see at that moment. Ryan looked at me, then at the principal, and then released me all at once. Both of us had been so wrapped up in the moment that we failed to notice the hush that had fallen on those remaining in the gym. The silence continued as we all filed into the classroom.

When we were back in our seats, Mr. Dunlap had an unpleasant surprise for us, another interrogation session of all the ninth- and tenth-graders. Using his getting-down-to-brass-tacks approach, he began.

"Ryan, did you touch those blinds in the library?" Ryan

immediately answered No. I felt a pang of disappointment shoot through me. Somehow, I had thought, I had hoped, that he was a truthful person.

Undaunted, Mr. Dunlap continued.

"Greg, did you touch those blinds in the library?"

Truthfully, Greg answered negatively.

"Edgar, did you touch those blinds in the library?" Mr. Dunlap's eyes were piercing, and Edgar's did not flicker. His conscience was clear.

"No, sir."

Then he proceeded with all the girls. When we all denied it he went back to the boys. After Edgar pleaded not guilty again Mr. Dunlap continued his badgering of Greg and Ryan, back and forth.

We sympathizers sat there with bated breath. If I could have done something—anything—to ease the situation a little I would have. My palms wasted no time getting into a nervous sweat and my stomach knot quickly formed.

For several minutes the two suspects maintained their innocence.

Then, with the wisdom that God gives to teachers, Mr. Dunlap eliminated Greg from his suspicions. Twice more he put the question to Ryan and twice more received a negative response. Then all at once we saw keys flying through the air toward Ryder and heard Mr. Dunlap's exasperated command:

"Ryan, go call your mother."

It took only a minute to figure out the implications. Stunned, I sat there in my seat, my heart in my throat. What should I think? Before I could answer that, my thoughts were interrupted by Ryan's voice.

"I didn't touch the blinds"—and then a pause, as if for final effect—"I touched the *cord!*"

The knot in my stomach untied and came raveling up into my throat in uncontrollable giggles. Up went my desk top, so I could escape Mr. Dunlap's piercing eyes and laugh in semi-privacy. What a riot! I thought. That Ryder had all the angles figured out—and he wasn't lying, after all. Relief swept over me like a cool breeze.

After a stern lecture in the office Ryan came back to the room to tell us goodbye. He would be suspended for three days this time. I groaned inwardly at the thought of his absence in the classroom. Three miserable days. I sent up a quick prayer that his mother wouldn't be too hard on him.

A PROBLEM
IN ALGEBRA

SEVERAL weeks had fled on wintery wings and semester exams were upon us. Mr. Dunlap gave us an open-book history test—and we thought we had it made. That is, we thought it would be easy until we began. The answers just weren't in the book, we were convinced.

At recess Kim and I got to discussing the questions that stumped us and made the happy discovery that each of us had the answers to the other's difficulties. Of course it wouldn't do to tell the answers. So we just kindly informed each other as to what page we found the particular answers on. (I was mortified that both questions that stumped me were about Ireland!) The action was justified we felt, due to the great difficulty and the fact that it was an open-book test.

So we reasoned, and a few more weeks went by.

The excitement of the holidays was far behind us now, and in the doldrums of very early spring we began to discuss more serious matters again. Kim and I again spoke our thoughts and ideas about being Christians. Kim's grandmother had given her a copy of *Messages to Young People,* and we began to read it up in Kim and Jeannie's room, when Jeannie was not there, of course. We didn't want her to think we were getting fanatical. We would take turns reading paragraphs out loud to each other. We covered several chapters, marking the lines that particularly impressed us.

We began to look forward to the coming of the Holley-Folkenberg team to hold a series of evangelistic meetings at our church. The excitement of a big series, coupled with Mr. Dunlap's standing offer of no homework on the nights we attended, convinced us that we would be in the gym for services each evening.

Algebra was giving us more than the usual difficulty these

days. We just could not figure out those horrid problems. It was such a chore to get the entire assignment done that we were very often *not* getting it done. In order to curb our negligence, Mr. Dunlap pursued a course of asking us if we had our algebra done before giving us permission to go out for recess. Now that softball season had begun for us, there was nothing more revolting than having to remain indoors and fidget over a series of problems that we had no idea how to solve.

And while I'm on the subject of algebra, let me mention something else. Young people, while not always setting high standards for themselves, are quick to censure their peers. One example of this occurred in algebra class.

We had the policy, "If you help me, I'll help you," when it came to algebra homework assignments. We figured that since the subject was so rough, if we were going to make it, we would have to band together. So Ryan, Kim, Karen, Greg, and I would take turns going to Mr. Dunlap's desk for help in solving the various problems. Then we would circulate the cards that Mr. Dunlap had worked the solution on, and hence all five of us would benefit. And Mr. Dunlap didn't seem to mind.

Now Edgar, it seemed, was never quite willing to ask for help himself, and yet he was always eager to get the solutions from us. Needless to say, it didn't set well with us—"the mighty five." We accused him of being a parasite and refused to give him answers, keeping them circulating within the boundaries of the "Fair Exchange Party Members" proper.

So Edgar began another method of chalking up algebra points. Until now he had appeared to be no smarter than the rest of us, but suddenly he was able to figure out all those hard problems. From whence came this remarkable ability?

I, being the nearest at hand, took upon myself the first step in solving the mystery, that of investigating the matter. When we began correcting our week's work on the next Friday, I propped myself up with my leg under me and peered over Edgar's shoulder to see, indeed, just what was going on.

I saw, for one thing, that there was absolutely no work

shown, a real no-no as far as Mr. Dunlap was concerned. All figuring was to be in evidence to the left of the column of answers. But that was a surprise; what came next was a real shocker. As Mr. Dunlap began reading off the algebra answers Edgar sat there writing them in! I suppressed a gasp as he marked a nice fat 100 percent at the top of the page. The mystery was solved.

And so the week's papers continued: Tuesday, 100 percent; Wednesday, 100 percent; Thursday, 100 percent; Friday, 97 percent.

Of all the nerve! I thought, but said nothing until I got together with the others after class. When the horrible truth came out, the five of us decided to take immediate action. Someone mentioned also that at the close of algebra class on the last several Fridays, Ed had rolled up his papers into a ball and placed them at the bottom of the trash on his way out to typing class.

We indignantly made our way back into the classroom and, rummaging around in the bottom of the trash can, uncovered Edgar's papers for the week. We crowded around as Ryan smoothed out the wrinkles, and the others saw that it was as I had said. Then, self-righteously, we paraded up to Mr. Dunlap's desk and turned over the evidence. Mr. Dunlap looked thoughtful and concerned. He took the papers from Ryan's hand and sent us to typing class with an "I'll take care of this matter, thank you."

We all felt justifiably indignant as we marched into the typing room with few words and many accusing looks. Edgar looked puzzled but said nothing.

The next morning found Mr. Dunlap, Elder Spencer, and Edgar within the confines of the office, but unfortunately for us interested ones the door was locked and the windows closed, with the curtains wide open so nobody could so much as even eavesdrop.

Several of us passed to the drinking fountain across from the office door several times to see if we could get any hints as to the

direction things were taking, but could hear nothing and could see only that the three of them looked very solemn.

Sometime later the trio emerged and Edgar returned to the classroom. It was obvious that he'd been crying, and I felt a bit sorry for him. He kept to himself pretty much after that, and never did he discuss what happened in the office that morning. We did notice, however, that from that time Edgar spent a lot of time doing algebra!

THE MAKING
OF A MONK

FOR some reason Kim stayed at Dunlap's one weekend rather than going home. We thought that was just great. Mr. Dunlap was probably thinking "great" too, only with a little different meaning, the poor man. But as someone once said, "There's no rest for the wicked, and the righteous don't need any." Mr. Dunlap was certainly righteous by our standards, and we just took his patience and toleration for granted.

That Sunday dawned gray and miserable. As the Dunlaps wouldn't let Kim stay overnight at my house (something we could *never* comprehend) we had persuaded Mrs. Dunlap to bring her over bright and early to spend the day. Upon her arrival we set off at once for the woods with a lunch in one hand and our walking sticks in the other. We were determined that weather should not spoil a chance to roam the back woods at will and dream and talk without fear of eavesdroppers. It's funny how we seemed to suspect others of the very things we were guilty of ourselves. In our excursions we found ourselves by a big dump. What fun it was to prowl through the mounds of debris and check things out.

Maverick would run up to the top of the larger piles of dirt and junk and stand there as if he were king of the mountain. We laughed at him. He lost a puppy tooth that day, which I carefully secured in the pocket of my jeans and later kept safe in a matchbox among my other treasures, such as Ryan's picture.

We finally reached a place we felt was secluded enough, found ourselves two good resting places, and whipped out the now-slightly-worn copy of *Messages to Young People*.

This evening would be the first of the Holley-Folkenberg meetings, and we were excited. After reading until certain parts of us fell asleep, we continued our journey. Lunch had been devoured during the reading session.

Our wanderings were at a slower pace after that as we

pondered aloud the thoughts that we had just exposed ourselves to. We were more convinced than ever that we would do something good for God. The question was, when?

We were following a creek that had grown too wide to jump. It was too wide for Kim, anyway. As for me, I gave a mighty leap and landed on the other side with only wet heels.

"Mighty Mouse is at it again," Kim commented half enviously as she tossed me the remains of our lunch, our walking sticks, and the *Messages to Young People.* At the last minute she lost her nerve for jumping and decided the best course would be to climb up a tree with an overhanging branch and go hand over hand to the other side.

When she was about midstream in her Tarzanlike passage, I got the urge to make a joke out of her semioverweight condition. Understand that to me an overweight person was anybody weighing more than one hundred pounds regardless of height. (I weighed eighty-nine at the time, remember? And Kim was about one hundred and forty. She thought I might blow away any minute and *never* thought of herself as overweight.) As she was moving along the branch I said aloud in very emphatic tones, "Snap!" Now, never before or since has this type of coincidence occurred in my life, but that day—I lie not—at the very *exact* instant that I voiced the word "Snap!" the branch broke with a loud crack and dropped Kim about five feet right into the icy-cold, rapidly flowing stream.

After one mouth-gaping moment of horror I launched into an uncontrollable fit of laughter. Both of us howled until tears streamed down our cheeks.

The next gust of the March wind, however, found Kim blue and shivering and the two of us hurrying for home still giggling. She was soaked to the skin and getting colder by the minute.

"Boy, I hope you don't get sick," I remarked as soon as I could get my breath.

"Oh, *I* won't get sick," she replied, emphasizing each word for effect. All winter long she'd run out to the car barefooted and jacketless to say goodbye when Maria came to pick me up, always insisting that *she* wouldn't get sick over little things like that, and, strangely enough, she never did.

"OK, Smarty—Old Lady Llewellyn wishes she'd been thrown in the watermelon this time! Sure would have been a lot warmer!" At that we clutched each other, weakened by a new attack of laughter.

While I found some of my mother's clothes for Kim we continued to giggle as we relived the entire episode. We couldn't wait to tell Ryan and Greg. As Kim dressed I picked up the scissors and began trimming my bangs a bit. A successful first attempt the week before had brought complimentary remarks from both my mom and Maria. So in an attempt to gain another bit of praise, I set about to do a replay of last week's efforts. While we were talking I kept on trimming.

"Whoops! A little too high on the left." So I began to level the right side off. Standing back for a critical look I noticed that now the right side was a littler shorter.

"Oh, dear," I fretted. "Have to even that up. Can't go to the meeting tonight looking like that." All the while I continued to gab with Kim. Finally I felt I had accomplished the task. I stood back to get Kim's affirmation on my hair-cutting skills.

"How does it look?"

"It looks OK." Dear old friend—she must have been looking beyond my hair. For neither of us seemed to notice that there was no more than an inch of the bangs remaining in any one spot.

Feeling quite pleased with myself, I dressed for the meeting. I wrote my mother a note saying that I had gone on to the meeting with Mrs. Dunlap and Kim and would meet her and Maria there. A quick stop by Dunlaps' so Kim could get into her own clothes and then we were on our way to the gym, where the meetings were to be held.

Some gracious women and a tall, good-looking man met us at the gym doors with Bibles and a punch card. They informed us that if we attended the meetings every night we could each receive a Bible at the end of the series.

Wonderful! we thought. We'll take it.

We found seats on the left side about halfway back and settled down for an interesting time of it, both hearing what the speaker had to say and also keeping a watchful eye on Ryan and Greg.

Preceding the meetings the Willow Run church members had tried an outreach program to encourage backslidden members who were a bit discouraged about one thing or another. Kim and I decided we would be a friendship team, as they called it, and signed up to visit someone on a friendly basis. Hopefully we would be able to encourage that person to attend the meetings.

We had been assigned to an elderly well-to-do woman who was bitter from some "run-ins" with one of the church pillars.

We had hopeful expectations of seeing her at the meeting that night. Scanning the audience we were disappointed when we failed to see her face. We exchanged glances with each other but said not a word.

By and by my mother and Maria sauntered in. They sat down near to where Greg and Ryan were sitting. Mother leaned forward on her chair as if to get a better look at us. A stern look passed over her face as she caught my eye for a brief moment.

"What's wrong?" Kim wondered aloud. She had noticed the look, too.

"I don't know. Maybe she's aggravated because I left the house early with you."

"Oh boy," Kim replied with that here-we-go-again sigh of hers. She crossed her arms decidedly and sat back in her chair.

Our thoughts were presently interrupted by the nice-looking man we had seen earlier. He strode up the steps confidently and took his place by the podium then he held a trombone up to his smiling face and played a beautiful tune that he afterwards announced would be the theme of the meetings. The words were in the front of the evangelistic hymnals that had been passed out at the door. He played the piece through again, and then we sang as he played it a third time. Kim and I loved the words and adopted them as our own theme song.

I've a longing in my heart for Jesus,

I've a longing in my heart to see His face;
I am weary, oh, so weary of trav'ling here below,
I've a longing in my heart for Him.

The message for the evening inspired us, and we began taking notes in the back of our Bibles. And we looked forward to the other meetings—no homework, a free Bible, lots of good music, and good news, plus a chance to see Ryan and Greg at night. Couldn't beat that.

Right after the meeting we got together with the boys for a few minutes of talk. It was the perfect ending to a happy day. Ryan was extra friendly that night, and I basked in the watchful gaze of his shining eyes. *He likes me,* I thought.

Maria had three passengers to take home, so we were quite a while getting to our place. Nothing was said about mother's stern look. That's good, I thought. I guess it wasn't anything important, after all.

But if I thought it would all blow over I had another think coming. We'd no sooner closed the front door behind us when she asked me a decidedly pointed question.

"What happened to your bangs?"

"Oh," I said, jerking up, and calling on my change-of-attitude tactic, "I gave them another trim. Don't they look nice?"

"Nice?"

"She looks like a monk," said Maria. She laughed at her own joke, hoping to break the tension of the situation. I did too.

"Well, she certainly can't go around with her hair like that," said mother in her no-nonsense tone. "Sit down, Marcie. I'll try to fix it up for you." And so saying she picked up the scissors and proceeded to cut my hair.

Tears stung my eyes as I felt the clipping around ear level. In no time she was done, and I glanced timidly in the mirror.

"Now what did you have to go and do that for?" I cried, bursting into a torrent of tears. I didn't wait for an answer but fled to my room, undressed, and flopped into bed.

"I do look like a monk now," I told myself, and cried till I slept.

ALMOST THE TEACHER

IF I was disappointed in my sudden change of appearance that night, things worsened considerably the next day. Everyone had their say about the new "Mighty Mouse look." All spoke frankly except Ryan, who had done a double take when he first saw me, but said nothing. I busied myself with studies the entire morning so I wouldn't have to think about it.

Finally in the typing room that afternoon Ryan confronted me, and in such a kind way. The others had gone back to the classroom. The door was locked as usual. I felt he still wanted to be alone with me in spite of my looks.

He moved up to the seat next to mine and sat facing me and the aisle. I nervously pecked away at the keys. Finally I stopped and regarded him.

"What'd she cut your hair for?" he asked almost tenderly with a note of agony in his voice.

"I don't know," I said half-disgusted and in desperation. "She aggravates me so much sometimes," I continued. The angry tone of mother's voice was still fresh in my memory.

"I know; so does mine. Well"—he paused and then went on in a tone that sounded half resigned and half hopeful—"at least it'll grow in again." And he winked at me.

A thrill passed through me. He winked at me! Did it really happen? Kim's right; he really does like me still. I was sure, after seeing my image in the mirror, that he would hate me. His wink at that moment meant more to me than any kiss. In a hasty attempt to keep from all but kissing *him* or at least grabbing his hand in admiration and relief, I began talking.

"Say, what did your mother ever do to you when you got kicked out that time?"

"Nothing. She just asked me what I did this time. And then she wouldn't let me ride my bike for a week."

"Oh, good!"

Then he reenacted the last time he had been expelled for three days the year before I came.

Laughter had come to his eyes by the time we heard the rattling of the keys. Back in the classroom Kim whispered to me.

"You must've had a good time."

"We did," I said, feeling justified in speaking for both of us. "But how could you tell?"

"Your eyes are shining!"

"Yours will be too when I tell you what happened." And we knuckled down to our studies.

But my mind kept drifting back to the incident in the typing room, and before I knew it, I was listening to the eighth-graders' science class. I'd had the same book the year before at the other school. They must have been afflicted with spring fever that afternoon also. The little group sat there staring blankly at Mr. Dunlap. When he asked a question their gaze would be immediately redirected to the open books before them with little or no change in expression. Occasionally Nettie fidgeted with a pencil and Lisa shuffled her feet around under the desk once or twice. Other than that it was just the humdrum of Mr. Dunlap's voice.

My mind drifted back to my Bible lesson. But every time Mr. Dunlap asked a science question, it would go unanswered and would divert my attention. Finally, I laid my pen aside and decided, If they won't answer the questions, I will.

So each time he asked a question, I answered. The remaining twenty minutes or so of the class time sped by. The rest of the day was uneventful until Mr. Dunlap—in a neutral tone of voice that gave not a hint as to his intentions—said he would like to see me in his office.

I gulped, and I'm sure my eyes must have widened considerably. My first thought was the typing room and that locked door. As Mr. Dunlap left his desk, I shot a quick glance back at Kim.

Her mouth closed and drew up into a tight side movement, and her eyebrows raised questioningly, as if to say, "You think my eyes would shine if I knew? What will his do?"

I looked beyond Kim to Ryan, who gave me a brief furrowed-eyebrow stare. I turned around and instinctively looked Karen's way—only to catch her snickering at me with dancing eyes; as if she knew all about the typing room (and perhaps a little more than Ryan and I did) as well as Mr. Dunlap's intentions of confrontation. That girl! It's a good feeling to be among friends when you're scared.

Next thing I knew I was perched, though not so jauntily as I would've liked to have been, on a chair opposite the desk, where Mr. Dunlap sat solemnly eyeing me, the poor Mighty Mouse.

"You were answering the questions that were intended for the eighth-graders' science class," said the teacher, after a moment. "You were to be studying your own material."

So it wasn't the typing room suspicions at all! Quickly I shifted gears and began to construct my defense.

"Well, I was bored, and they weren't paying any attention, so I thought I'd help them out."

The discussion became a bit heated, and then Mr. Dunlap asked, "Do you want to teach the class?" never supposing, of course, that I would take him up on it.

But my dander was up now and I wasn't about to back down. The big scare was over, and I had to have something significant to report to the others.

"Yes, I'll teach," I came back.

"All right," he said quietly. "You will take over the eighth-grade science and Bible class tomorrow afternoon." He rose to his feet, which terminated the discussion. I dropped by the water fountain before making my triumphant entry into the classroom. I was conscious of all eyes upon me as I walked, head erect, to my seat. Curious eyes they were, searching but in vain for some clue as to what had happened. I proceeded to prepare my things to take home and set my desk in its final order for the day, avoiding all stares. It would have a more dramatic effect, I thought.

We sang one stanza of "Turn Your Eyes Upon Jesus" and Gregory said a prayer, and we were out the door and down the hall. They plied me with questions, but I waited till we were out the front door before I launched into what had happened. When I climaxed the account with my agreement to take over the teaching next day, Karen said, "Did you really?"

I nodded my head quite nonchalantly and walked on. The response had been grand. To celebrate my new position as eighth-grade school marm Kim and I made a left at the main road and walked on into the town part of Willow Run. We sang the length of Main Street until we came to the stores. We stopped in to see the monkey in the locksmith's shop. But our true mission urged us on before long, and we continued to the delicatessen and bought some candy bars. Stuffing them into our pockets, we strolled on over to the railroad tracks, and seating ourselves high on the abandoned station platform we let our legs dangle with the two loafers and two desert boots kicking at the wooden beams below. We discussed the day's events and eventually got to the typing practice.

"Can you believe he actually winked at me? I thought he'd never even look at me again after that haircut."

"Well, you know he likes you, and so does everyone else know it. That's why Kathy doesn't warm up to you—because she liked him the year before." Blessed confirmation. Even a monk's haircut couldn't daunt my spirit of peace.

We mosied on to Dunlaps' and talked with Greg until Maria came. The evangelistic meeting was good that night also. I thought Ryan and Greg would sit with us, but they didn't. And it was with great glee that we saw Sister Elmhurst, our friendship team contact, that evening. The sermon was excellent, and we felt sure she would be there after that. We felt quite confident in our get-them-to-come-back abilities and were about ready to ask for another name to visit.

The next day as soon as school began I walked briskly up to Mr. Dunlap's desk and in a very businesslike manner proceeded to ask him for a textbook with which to prepare for each of the classes that I was to be in charge of. At my proposal, a troubled look crossed his face. He shook his head and said, "I've changed my mind. I'll do the teaching today." So I was still a student after all.

In typing class we were given a speed and accuracy test. At the end of three minutes, Mrs. Dunlap asked us to tally up the mistakes and the number of words per minute we had typed. Karen, as we sometimes called her, was at the top with fifty-seven words per minute and only two mistakes. I was doing considerably worse with forty-seven words per minute and three mistakes. Kim was about the same, and Edgar and Ryan didn't do too badly, considering. Then it came Gregory's turn. We had to wait for another tabulation and then his announcement: twenty-seven words and sixteen mistakes. Of course we all laughed. Poor Greg! But sweet Mrs. Dunlap, who could type eighty words a minute, comforted him:

"You may be a slower typist, Greg, but you could put us all to shame taking an engine apart." Greg beamed. It was true.

At lunchtime Edgar was his usual pesky self. He could be so aggravating sometimes. He would turn around and take a bite out of his sandwich and then hold it over my glass of milk and, tapping it with his ring finger, let the crumbs drop in my milk. It had happened many times before. He knew it got my goat.

"Edgar, cut it out," I demanded. To which he only laughed. Tension had been building on this point for days, and it finally came to a head.

After lunch period we prepared to go out for recess. Only Ryan, Edgar, and I remained in the room with Mr. Dunlap, who was absorbed in some reading material as he finished his lunch. Edgar made some half-joking remark to me to which I had a sassy reply.

Ryan looked at Edgar icily and told him to watch who he was talking to, which only triggered another smart remark from Ed. Then like two quarrelsome kittens they were into it. In the short scuffle Edgar lost his glasses, though fortunately, they didn't break. Before Mr. Dunlap looked up, it was over and we three were out the door. I guess he just figured "Boys!" and let it go at that.

Once outside we had a lively game of dodge ball, and I basked in the happy knowledge that Ryan had taken up for me.

"He was so noble," I sighed aloud.

"What's that?" said Lisa.

"Oh, nothing," I said and darted after the ball.

That afternoon in typing practice more almost-completed papers got torn out of the typewriters than usual. One of us would discover somebody was ahead, and before you knew it someone else had snatched the fast person's work out of the typewriter and wadded it up. The muffled laughter continued most of the period. As I was nearing my next-to-last line Edgar ripped my paper out and destroyed it. But he had had his pulled out twice, so I didn't feel so bad.

By and by I found myself totally alone, pecking away at my practice sheet. It wasn't long before Greg made his appearance. This was a bit unusual, but I brightened at the prospect of company. He sat down across from me and smiled.

"Hi, Tidge."

"Hi. What's on your mind?"

"Well," he said, "the youth rally is coming up in Windsor next month, and it'll be an all-day affair. I was wondering if you and Ryan would like to sit with Kathy and me? Well, what I mean is, would you like to go with Ryan? Then all four of us could run around together."

A surge of confused excitement shot through me. But I, usually so quick with a smart remark, was completely blank now. Only later was I able to sift things out and formulate the questions I wanted to ask Greg. Why didn't Ryan ask me himself? Was this a date? What did Greg think Ryan thought of me? Did he ask Greg to ask me?

All I could manage besides breaking into a cold sweat was a smile and a "Yes, I'll be glad to go."

And with a "Thanks, Tidget" he was off.

I sat there staring at the typewriter as if it were a new and fascinating animal. Now I could see why Ryan left early—he had

no doubt put Greg up to asking me. I daydreamed about parading around the stadium holding hands with Ryan. I wished it would be Kim, and not Katharine, who would be accompanying Greg. A whole month seemed like an eternity to wait.

Greg and Ryan were standing by the corner in the hallway talking. I thought Ryan looked a little sheepish, but Greg played the part of gracious go-between, and soon we were all three gabbing and cutting up. Finally, Kim came for a drink and to tell us that Mr. Dunlap was waiting for us, so we reluctantly returned to the classroom and tried to be studious.

A GREAT
FALL

THE days sped by, each filled with the fun of being young and happy. Occasionally after school Kim, Greg, and I would hop on our bikes and take to the country roads surrounding Willow Run. What fun we had, and our talks brought a closeness among us that was not soon forgotten. How much we treasured those days of serene calm mixed with carefree fun and mischief!

Life was good. And that time, as I look back on it, holds a special meaning—almost like a golden era. The setting of those days can never be relived. People and places change so much. Children grow up soon enough and must cope with the ever growing responsibilities and more complicated situations that come with passing years. But those carefree days were giving us a background that would strengthen us for the complexity of life and its problems.

Our close bond of friendship no doubt shone through in our everyday relationships in the classroom. Perhaps it was this that led Katharine to extract a solemn vow from Greg that he would not speak to me under any circumstances.

Understand it I could not. What had happened to jovial Greg? As fate would have it, word came through the grapevine, and I could see the real issue at stake. But I had no understanding of the insecurity that racked Katharine. What in the world is she jealous of? I pondered to myself. Can't she understand a brother-sister relationship?

So, gone were the days when Greg, Kim, and I would play hide-and-seek at Dunlaps' and Greg would hide me in the hamper or under the piano or in a dark cubbyhole upstairs.

I felt a bit of rejection for a day or so, but everyone else's attitude seemed unchanged toward me, particularly Ryan's, so I decided to shrug it off. And the days ahead provided plenty of diversion.

Working on MV Honors, Kim and I got involved in collecting bugs for our Insect Honor. Recesses and free periods found us out scanning the fields for bugs of every description. We found many to add to our ever growing collections. Again, as with the reading time spent with library books, we thought we were getting away with murder as we idled away the hours seeking our own pleasure. But the lessons we learned as we observed nature further acquainted us with the Maker of all things. We were constantly marveling at the variety and beauty of the insects we found in the area encircling the school.

Another highlight in our curriculum was preparing for the upcoming athletic meet with the other church schools in the district. Mr. Dunlap read us a list of the planned events. Kim and I decided to practice up for the three-legged race and a few other things.

Practice was fun. Standing side by side, we would tie a scarf around our adjacent legs, combining them into a single "leg." From the start we found it easy to coordinate our movements so as to be in step with each other. And this state of three-leggedness began to demonstrate itself in many of our activities. When we walked home from school to Dunlaps', we made the trip on three legs. When we left the meeting at the gym in the evening, round the anklebones would go the scarf, and we'd remain that way until Maria picked me up.

As the old saying goes, "Practice makes perfect," and we were no exception to the rule. In the days that followed we perfected our act to the point that we put other aspiring three-leggers in our school to shame.

One night we even went to visit a sick friend in the hospital on three legs. We untied ourselves at the elevator and paid our brief visit. Back in the hall, we tethered ourselves together once again and continued on our way. We were going to win that race and that was all there was to it. We could jog around the block in record time and do hopping and skipping stunts. We were quite pleased with ourselves.

These activities helped to blot out the hurt of being ignored by Gregory. He was following Katharine's instructions well. Kim and I were somewhat surprised when he approached us one day after school. We had replenished our candy bar supply at the deli and were on another excursion to the railroad tracks to talk. We delayed there some time and then strolled toward the creek. As we started back to Dunlaps', we were approached from behind by a cyclist. Automatically we moved to one side as we heard the bike approaching. Our attention was attracted when the rider slowed down and we heard a familiar voice pose the question:

"Where have you two been? How about a ride?"

I glanced back to see if my ears were playing tricks—was that really Gregory's voice? Indeed, it was. Kim and I kept on walking.

"Hey, Tidget, aren't you going to talk to me?" At this I wheeled around to face him.

"Me talk to you? I thought that was against your scruples."

"Hers, not mine. I've had enough, and I'm going to tell her tomorrow."

"Oh," I said, for once doing more thinking than talking, "so the bird is out of his cage."

"It's about time," Kim ventured.

"Yeah, well," Greg remarked, "if she gives me a hard time about it I'm gonna tell her to forget it. Now are you going to let me give you a ride or not?"

A weight seemed to be lifted from me. I felt freer than I had been for days. Though I hated to admit it, Greg's aloofness bothered me not a little. I broke into a smile of gratitude and relief.

"Sure," I said. "Why not?" Kim parked herself on the back fender and I took the place that I usually occupied when things were crowded—on the handlebars. Perched there I wanted to shout and sing. Instead, we all talked a blue streak.

Needless to say, things took a turn for the worse the next day. Greg had called Katharine when we got back that day and she had laid down the law and hung up. During school I received more than my share of glares from a certain person. But the jokes and banter in general continued.

I'll be glad when this blows over, I thought more than once.

Personal problems were for the most part forgotten, however, in the bustle of preparing for the sports meet between Willow Run and other schools in the district. The day arrived, dawning sunny and clear. We piled into several cars and drove to the Windsor church. The sports events and picnic lunch would be held on the grounds there.

I felt a bit uncomfortable among so many strangers. Kim was fairly well acquainted with a number of the youth who attended church in Windsor and who had gotten special permission to be excused from public schools to attend the gala affair. Scott Kaiser was there, much to my secret delight.

Sack races, standing broad jumps, and relay races took place amid shouts and cheers. It was great fun and we didn't do too badly.

"Just wait for 'our' race," said Kim. "We'll show them."

We had a nice picnic lunch with plenty to eat. That out of the way, Kim and I practiced a bit for the three-legged race, which was scheduled first thing after lunch. Very confidently we tied the scarf for the last time and strode up to the starting line.

But in the excitement of the day we had forgotten to decide which foot we would start off on, the middle one or the outside ones. Fatal mistake. The whistle was blown and off we started—on two different feet. There was a mad scramble, and we both landed in a heap just over the starting line. We were mortified—everyone else had left us behind in the dust, and there was no use trying to catch up now despite the urging of Mr. Dunlap and Trudy. In our embarrassing predicament we reverted to our tried and true protection—laughing. So there we lay on the ground cackling away the tension our spill had created. We were terribly disappointed that it should end like this after all those weeks of diligent practicing. It seemed totally unfair. Surely they would do a retake. But Mr. Dunlap was displeased with both of us. After allowing us so much time to practice he had expected a better performance than this disgraceful scene at the starting line.

In the process my shoe had come off and a dime I had in hiding went flipping up into the air, the sight of which made us laugh all the harder. Tears rolled down our cheeks, and every time we'd look at each other we would crack up again.

Trudy understood our predicament and joined in the hilarity, but Mr. Dunlap's face remained stern.

Then there was the softball game for the boys. Kim, Karen, and I sat on the sidelines laughing, cutting up, and making jokes all the way through it. During the seventh-inning stretch we slipped off to a nearby ice-cream stand and purchased cones.

It had been a funny day for us, tragic in the respect that all our practicing had been in vain. But it was one day that we would not soon forget.

THE GREAT REFORMATION

ANOTHER of those rare weekends when Kim could stay over was approaching. We looked forward in eagerness to it.

Being the church librarian, I scurried into the library area between Sabbath school and church on Sabbath morning. It was my duty to open things up in case anyone wanted books. Thus occupied, I failed to notice some members from the Windsor church coming in the front door.

Kim had followed me into the office and we were chattering as usual.

"Well," I said, "I want to go say Hi to my 'mother-in-law' for a minute." I made ready to dash into the crowded corridor.

Kim injected, "Maybe you mean *Fran's* mother-in-law."

I shot a glance at her to read the real significance of her words, if there indeed was any. Out in the hall my fears deepened. There they were talking together, Fran and Ryan. My stomach coiled into its knot.

Who does she think she is anyway? I thought. Of all the nerve!

All during church I was troubled by scary feelings. They sat together, and my heart bled. Kim sat with me for consolation. Whipping out the bulletin and taking a pen from Maria's purse I asked Kim on paper:

"What's she doing here anyhow?"

Kim wrote back, "She got sick and had to leave TDA (a boarding academy in another State)."

"Oh, brother!" I retorted. "Isn't she going back?"

"I don't know," she replied on paper. "I don't think so, though."

I groaned inwardly. Would this be the end of my relationship with Ryan? My weekend was totally ruined.

Kim came to our house for dinner. After helping with the

dishes we took Maverick out for a long walk, and she and I had a long talk.

Fran, it seemed, had quite a bit of confidence regarding her ability to attract boyfriends. And her self-confident manner evidently inspired confidence in Ryan that he otherwise lacked. I had noticed a troubled look on Trudy's face as the two of them left church together.

My world seemed to be caving in on me.

"Now I wonder about the youth rally."

"Oh, he'll probably be over her by then. You still have a week to work your charms."

I felt little consoled, and well I might, as Monday morning brought an obvious aloofness from Ryan that I couldn't deny. I was crushed. How could he be like that? I asked myself the question over and over again.

The week dragged by. I hurried as fast as I could to get my typing practice sheet done so as not to have to remain alone with him. How I wished that he would grab me and pull me close and say to me that he really didn't care about her, that it was nothing, and that he really loved me.

But he didn't, and in the distress of that week I took to the back woods with Maverick to relive the scenes again and again. How could he do this to me? If I could have cried my heart might have healed more quickly. But the hurt was too deep down for me to cry it out, and besides crying showed weakness and I wasn't weak. At least that's what I had been brought up to believe.

"All right, Mr. Branson," I stated firmly to Maverick late one afternoon. "You just go ahead and like her and hurt me. *Try* to hurt me, and I won't let you know, even if it kills me. I can be just as proud and arrogant as you can. Two can play the same game, you know. Just you wait and see."

Rising from my log, I strode back home. I would admit to no one, with the exception of Kim, that I still liked him. As far as the world was concerned, my feelings for Ryan were dead and would remain so. Self-defense barriers were being built, and no

one but Ryan himself would be able to knock them down. The cold war had begun.

The Holley-Folkenberg meetings had been over for several weeks now, and Kim and I decided finally to follow through on our plans to reform. One night after prayer meeting we made our way over to Dunlaps'. We had left immediately after the benediction in order to accomplish as much as we could before Maria came to pick me up. We felt our way through the dark living room, refraining from turning on lights till we reached the upstairs.

As we neared the top of the steps we suddenly heard a roar and nearly jumped out of our skins. Greg had crouched on the stairs, lying in wait for us, and he struck at precisely the right moment. Kim screamed. I felt my heart leap up into my throat and settle back into place. I didn't make a sound; I couldn't for a few seconds. Then the three of us began to laugh, especially Greg. That boy!

The scare over, we scampered up the rest of the way and took out our *Messages to Young People,* some notebook paper, and a pen.

"Well, where shall we begin?"

"Why don't we read and list things as we go that we need to improve on?"

"That sounds good, and then maybe we could make up a chart to help us keep track."

"Great! And why don't we pick names for our reformation?"

"OK." Our enthusiasm was growing. There was a pause, and then I said, "I have my name picked out—I'll be Martha Luther."

"Oh, neat. Who shall I be? I'll be Mrs. Wycliffe—Jane Wycliffe."

"Oh, cool! And we can write our names on the top of our charts."

"Yes, let's do." And so it was decided that I was Martha and she was Jane.

As we read through the well-marked sections of *Messages to Young People* we jotted down our areas of weakness. The list grew alarmingly. Before Maria arrived it was of a length that would have discouraged would-be saints with lesser enthusiasm.

As usual, Maria came all too soon. By the next day, however, we had perfected our list and set about making charts. Mr. Dunlap lent some colored pencils for our project. The days of the week went across the top and the things we wanted to work on went down the page. Under the chart itself we wrote James 4:7, 8 in our best writing: "Submit yourselves therefore to God. Resist the devil, and he will flee from you. Draw nigh to God, and he will draw nigh to you."

Some of the things we included on the charts were: eating between meals, wearing pants all the time, respecting parents and other adults, using time wisely, eating sweets, doing home-work, studying the Sabbath school lesson and *Messages to Young People,* overcoming temper, and forming good grooming habits. Completing the charts gave us real satisfaction. We felt relieved to be on our way to "being good." How the human heart longs to be right with God. We didn't understand at the time that we only needed a daily relationship with our heavenly Father and that He would work with us on the rest. That was what drawing nigh to God was all about. Our knowledge was small but our efforts were earnest.

Each day we noted our progress, or lack of it, and talked and prayed together. We felt so good about everything, and our relationship deepened.

As we continued our praying and reading we felt impressed to confess some of the sins of greater magnitude. Again we made up lists and checked them off as we scurried here and there making things right. Kim took her list home with her one weekend and I wrote several letters to finish off mine. One of the dreaded things was that open-book history exam on which we had exchanged page numbers. We felt that confession was part of being good, and if that's what it took, that's the way it would be. So one afternoon we went to Mr. Dunlap's desk just before the bell rang to come back in from recess. (We figured if we waited till after recess to tell him he would take up world history time talking to us in the office rather than valuable recess time.)

Mr. Dunlap regarded our sober countenances with a questioning look, but asked not a word as to our mysterious intentions. He nodded his head and said he would see to it that we could talk to him during the next period. With a timid "thank-you" we fled for the bathroom, where we attempted to polish up our confession.

The bell rang and we nervously reentered the classroom, oblivious to the chatter about us. After giving the various classes their assignments, we heard the now familiar jangle of the keys.

"OK, Marcie and Kim, if you'll come with me——" Mr. Dunlap's voice trailed off as he led the way out into the hall. Kim and I obediently rose and followed him out the door. Ryan shot a shocked and questioning expression at me as I passed by. I only made a face at him and kept on going.

Let him suffer in wonderment, I thought. Serves him right.

Once in the office Mr. Dunlap offered us two chairs. I immediately collapsed into one of them. It had been decided that

Kim would ask for the appointment and I would begin the confession session, and then we would play it by ear after that. I drew a deep breath, as one in great pain might, and opened my mouth. Mr. Dunlap looked at me expectantly, but nothing came out.

"Wait a minute," I said, and he very graciously fiddled with some papers on the desk in an attempt to set me at ease.

All at once I had an overwhelming urge to go to the bathroom. "Oh, dear," I told myself, "surely not now." Bracing myself on the edge of my chair—which I hoped he interpreted as nothing but a "get set" action, I began my speech.

"Well, Kim and I are trying to do what's right, and we happened to think back to the open-book history test we took and we thought we'd better tell you that we cheated on it. And we're sorry."

There—it was said. But oh, how terrible the bare facts sounded.

"So you're sorry you cheated on the history exam?" he repeated contemplatively.

"Well," said Kim, automatically rising to our defense, "we didn't copy answers. We just helped each other out with the page numbers."

"I see." Mr. Dunlap looked away from us and down at the desk. "Well, it is an honorable thing to confess our sins," he said, playing with the paper clip container with both hands. He cleared his throat. "How many answers did you give each other page numbers for?"

"Two each," blurted out Kim, who was by this time in tears.

Oh, no, I thought. What's she crying for? And then I thought, *Oh, dear.* If I don't cry maybe he won't believe I'm sincere. (As if shaking like a leaf wouldn't convince him!) So I sat there and tried to think of something—anything over which I could shed a few tears. I thought of my Aunt Mag's funeral a while back. No good. I didn't even cry then. How could I produce tears over it now? Over Ryan? No, I was too stubborn for that. My dad? That was it. I thought of the family and my eyes filled immediately. I began to sniff. Ah, there, that's better. That sounds more like it.

Now what was he saying? Something about prayer?

"I think it would be appropriate to pray and ask the Lord's forgiveness."

Neither Kim nor I had the gumption at this point to inform him we already had. So with heads bowed we each reinformed the Lord of our trespasses, and then Mr. Dunlap offered a prayer of thankfulness for "these two dear girls who are trying to do Your will" and that God would "please help them in their endeavors along the Christian pathway."

Then came the announcement we had been hoping for all along.

"I don't believe we'll need to alter the grades any this time—I know you won't do it again, and you've been doing extra outside work with those reports."

"Whew," we sighed in unison. We'd had visions of failing history for the term. I suppose that was what made me so nervous.

Another timid "Thank you" escaped from the two of us. Once out of the office we again sought refuge in the bathroom, as Mr. Dunlap had given us permission to freshen up before returning to the classroom.

"He's not so bad after all, is he?" I remarked.

"He'll do," retorted Kim in mock disgruntlement. At that we cracked up laughing, and the tension of the last half hour seemed to melt away.

Kim stood there wiping her eyes. "You're lucky you wear glasses."

"Well, what did you go and cry for, anyway, Old Lady Llewellyn?"

"I couldn't help it—I noticed you weren't so dry-eyed yourself!"

"I felt obligated after you started. I was afraid he'd think you meant it and I didn't." This inspired more peals of laughter. With this we tiptoed rather exaggeratedly into history class. But

solemn indeed was my determination never to cheat again, *ever!*
There would be no more confession sessions like this for me. It
wasn't worth the mental agony.

The youth rally came, and Kim and I attended together.
After the picnic dinner we slipped off with our *Messages to Young
People* and read and talked and compared our charts. We were a
bit discouraged about Sister Elmhurst. We had made our Tuesday afternoon visits faithfully, but there were no apparent
results. We prayed about it, and then let the matter drop. Ryan
was at the youth rally with Fran Cooper, and Greg was very
attentive to Betty, whom he had liked the year before. Kim and I
saw the four of them often during the day, and the sight was a
real thorn in our flesh.

The highlight of the day came when we unexpectedly saw
Tony there. Tony DiAngelo was a handsome Italian who had
loved my sister from the time she was sixteen. He was on leave
from the Army for his dad's funeral. Mr. DiAngelo had died of a
heart attack, but even this sadness couldn't keep Tony's happy
nature from bubbling through. I ran up and hugged him, and he
invited me to ride back to Willow Run and go shopping with
him.

He turned to Kim and said, "Oh, this is your friend Slim!"
Kim looked at him with a reprimanding look.

"Oh, it's not Slim? Oh, then it's Flim." We burst into
laughter.

I felt proud when at the close of the rally I walked out arm in
arm with Tony. He was *so* good-looking and a real "hunk," as we
categorized fellows with an impressive physique. I hoped Ryan
had seen.

The shopping spree was great. We had such a good time
together. Later, sitting on the edge of the front seat in his new
Falcon and gazing out the window, I thought to myself:

I do hope Maria decides to marry him. Already I loved him as
a big brother.

"What are you thinking that calls for such seriousness?" He

interrupted my silent run of thoughts.

"Oh," I confessed, "I do hope Maria decides to marry you."

He smiled and sighed, "Well, why don't you try to convince her. Seems like I'm not doing a very good job."

"I will." And then I added to myself, *I must.* But I would have to figure out a way to proceed.

EPISTLES AND THE MUTE CONTEST

RYAN was obviously angry at me Monday morning. Perhaps he had seen me leave the youth rally with Tony, or maybe he was upset that I hadn't pursued him when Fran turned up on the scene. At any rate, he was out of sorts and I wasn't about to inquire why. I just tuned him out. Seems like I did a lot of that lately.

April was nearing its end, and I had been informed that my mother and I would be leaving for the Midwest in August. I had had my heart all set on another year in Willow Run, and now those dreams were being shattered. I felt resentful.

Ground had been purchased halfway between Windsor and Willow Run, and the two churches would cooperate in building one church school. I would miss our little school. Kim and Greg would no longer have to stay with Dunlaps but would ride the minibus that would be purchased as things progressed.

In an attempt to hold on to the world that had grown dear to me, I began writing an epistle to Kim. (Since we always liked to use big words we often called a letter an epistle. We liked the way it sounded.) All the treasured memories of the past year were ingrained in my brain, and I wanted to make sure they remained as important to her. The epistle ran like this:

April 19, 1966

In Memory of Our Ninth Grade Together.

THE EPISTLE OF MIGHTY MOUSE

Dear Fink (Rat),

I'll never forget your corny face and disposition. I s'ppose you'll never ever forget me, either—and Maverick!

Boy, we got away with murder *sometimes*, didn't we? But we sure had a lot of fun. Especially at Ingathering. I'll never forget the time we slipped trying to run to one side of the street. (I won anyway!) The money went everywhere. What a mess!!! I still have the bruise (Ha! Ha!). I guess you do too.

Don't ever forget our code: YEOTUV ATRLEO RPEKAI-LELUY AT REAITVFOIENQK!! All the notes we passed—it's a wonder we didn't get bawled out in the office. Oh, well!

I keep telling you not to forget some of the things we did, but all the algebra we had this year ruined our brains so that we probably won't remember anything—except perhaps all the boring history classes we sat through. By the way, "Mabel," will you help me diagram some sentences after we come in from recess? (Only kidding, of course.)

And, too, I mustn't forget our "dear" typing class and all the blasts we had in that room. (And all the mischief we got into.)

Oh, yes, and all our noteworthy sayings, our communing on the telephone, all our Monopoly games and sit-ups. Then there was putting up with a living parasite (you-know-who), walking around the block umpteen times, *suffering*, trying to keep a chart of high standards, Jane and Martha, and all the hikes we took.

One thing I know you will never forget—algebra or no algebra—is "SNAP!" I guess I needn't go into it; you know the story backwards. Well, I'd better be going now. 'Bye-eee.
P.S. A matter of fact—Irish are better than Welsh, and Gallagher is better than Llewelyn!

Lots of luv,
Mighty Mouse
(The magnificent)

Kim's reaction was all I hoped for, and all through the afternoon study period she bent ardently over her notebook writing nonstop until her reply was completed. We spent typing practice typing them up for each other. Kim's contained these thoughts:

April 19, 1966
In Memory of Our Ninth Grade Together
THE EPISTLE OF RAT FINK

Dear Mighty Mouse,

Although we have suffered all year through the realms of history class and the arguments of algebra class we must admit we had fun!

Boy, what fun we had at recess! I'll never forget your mighty efforts to get the ball over the net in volleyball. (Were you learning to fly?)

Sure, I'll help you diagram those sentences after recess if you'll give me a nice box of chocolates to nibble on in exchange. (How funny!)

Yes, we got away with murder most of the time. By the way, who fixed the ripped dollar bill on *our* annual dollar night? Is your skirt still wet? Is Brother Oglethorpe still your best friend? OK. OK. I'll stop there, but Ingathering sure was a lot of fun!!!!!!!

You're asking why my ear looks so funny? Well, it's still cauliflowered from our last telephone conversation.

Hey, hey, you worm, you had better watch out in the years to come whose plants you feed on. They may not be as generous as Mr. Dunlap was. (That plant *was* good, though, huh?)

Ouch!!! What's the matter? Well, I'm still suffering from those 215 smacks you gave me on my 15th birthday! (They hurt! You little bully.)

My note of advice: Now, now, Martha, don't forget the high standards we set during our GREAT REFORMATION!!!

Though your brain be stretched from algebra never forget the "big-mouthed Rat Fink." I'll always remember you.

With all my nerve,
Rat Fink

P.S. A matter of opinion—FORD IS BEST! A matter of fact—Llewellyn is spelled with four l's.

'Bye-eeeeeeeeeeeeeeee

We were so pleased with what we had written that we decided to see if we could get a whole collection of them together. That evening after supper, and indeed many evenings thereafter, we sat on either end of the telephone line, pen in hand, poring over dictionaries from which to abstract words (Kim with a Webster's and I with a medical one).

We tried different combinations and laughed till tears rolled down our cheeks. When we hit a combination that struck our fancy we'd write it down and go on to the next, until either Maria or Mr. Dunlap would insist that we get off the phone. It was Mr. Dunlap who teasingly suggested that we would get cauliflowered ears from spending too much time on the phone.

It was debatable as to whether or not our writings made sense, but our 14-year-old minds thought they were grand. (Excuse me, Kim had had her fifteenth birthday and was my senior now, at which time she demanded that I have respect for my elders. In my attempts to get even, I reminded her on appropriate occasions that she would be an old hag six months before me!) We set out to memorize some choice parts and stage a sort of drama, much like two old cats on the back fence, in which we would bicker back and forth.

Time continued to pass and with it Ryan's fling with Fran. He began breaking down the wall that had grown between the two of us. And it didn't take getting down on his hands and knees. I was ready for the reconciliation. There was nothing dramatic about it; he just came in one morning acting friendly and I was friendly right back. It was a good feeling to be at peace with Ryan again. The world seemed a warmer place.

At lunch one day the subject came up of who was the more incessant talker, or which of us had the least amount of self-control—Kim or me. Of course, each of us had a goodly amount of confidence in herself along such lines, and each stoutly defended her honor. The outcome resulted in a "mute contest" to see who could go the longest without talking. What a painful afternoon it was for both of us, I'm sure. The gift of speech is very precious to teen-agers.

When school ended for the day, we were still not speaking, but we left together and headed for Dunlaps'. It was decided through mental telepathy to play Monopoly—mutely of course.

That night at supper my mother got a bit perturbed at my silence, but she brightened up when it came time for dishes. Without a word of protest I launched into the task at hand. And the telephone line was clear all evening.

The next morning a note I had taped on the mirror reminded me that the contest was still on. At school things were again quiet. It was getting rather tiresome.

But Kim hadn't opened her mouth and spoken yet, and I wasn't about to be a quitter. The morning dragged by. Mrs. Dunlap smiled in amusement when Greg's aggravations proved unsuccessful in getting Kim to voice her disgust at him.

Lunch hour passed and Kim and I were surrounded with much discussion regarding competitive sports. We listened but said nothing. Library books were never so appreciated. They took the strain off remembering not to talk.

History period rolled around. Mr. Dunlap calmly proceeded with his occasional alternate to teaching—having each student read a section aloud. My heart jumped to my throat when he called Karen, the bowlegged, long-necked heron (as we called her sometimes, despite the fact that she was none of these). Karen, then Jeannie and Greg, then who? Would he come up our row from the back or start with Edgar up front? It was crucial because it would determine the outcome of the contest—or would it? While my thoughts turned over in my mind I heard his selection.

"All right, Edgar, continue reading."

That meant I was next. All the eighth-graders' eyes were upon me, waiting for my certain doom. My stomach tensed with excitement. Without even thinking, I was out of my seat and all but running to the chalkboard to sign out. I figured if I looked urgent enough I could get by with it.

As Edgar droned on, I sought refuge in the restroom.

Poor Kim, I thought. But rather her than me.

Later, when I was sure Edgar had finished, I sauntered out of the restroom and stole softly to the door. My ear to the crack, I could hear Ryan's monotone and felt quite safe to enter. Like an Olympic champion I made my entrance. I floated over to take my place, and even Kim's shaking her fist at me in mock anger didn't phase me. That, coupled with the looks on the faces of my classmates, told me that my action had saved the day—for me, at least. I was the uncontested winner of the mute contest.

LITTLE CALAMITIES, NEW YORK STYLE

MAY was well under way when the day of the class trip to New York City finally arrived. We were up early that Tuesday morning. The class trip was a much-looked-forward-to event, and my stomach was caught up in the swing of things with its usual knot.

We would go in two cars—Mr. Dunlap's and Trudy Branson's. Kim and I had already decided who would be going with whom and felt quite fortunate when things worked out that way.

The day dawned clear and mild. By seven o'clock we were all gathered in front of Dunlaps'. The eighth-graders and Jeannie and Edgar went with Mr. Dunlap, and Ryan, Kim, Greg, Karen, and I piled into Trudy's Buick. We weren't even out of the Willow Run city limits before the cutting up began. But almost at once we realized that Ryan was in another of his give-me-a-hard-time moods, and Greg seemed to follow suit. Kim gave me one of her why'd-they-have-to-pick-today looks, and we both settled back to ignore them. We were disgusted over the fact that they sat up front with my "mother-in-law."

But just because those two weren't in a good mood didn't mean they had intentions of leaving us alone. We bickered happily on many topics, including the merits of Fords and the demerits of Chevies and Buicks and vice versa. One thing followed another the entire way to New York.

If we girls tried to sleep, the boys would bug us, and if we tried to hold a conversation among ourselves, they would invariably break in with their saucy remarks. "No rest for the weary," we sighed more than once.

After what seemed an eternity we arrived in the city. Plans for the day included visits to the Statue of Liberty and the Empire State Building, a ferry ride to Staten Island, with a picnic lunch in one of the many city parks.

Delighted at the happy prospects we climbed out of the car,

merged with the rest of the class and were soon caught up in the crowds making their way to the Empire State Building. What had begun as a bright day gradually turned to dismal gray, and then rain started a gentle pitter-patter.

Coming up the street on which stood the magnificent Empire State Building, we gasped as we imagined we saw it swaying back and forth in the wind. I wasn't sure that I wanted to go up there. A bit disconcerted, I put on my calm cover-up act and approached Mr. Dunlap.

"How long has this building been here?" I queried.

"It was completed back in 1931."

"Oh," I said. And then to myself, Well, if it has stood swinging and swaying in the breeze this long, I guess it'll hold another half hour or so until we get in to see it. Thus convincing myself I proceeded to go through the revolving doors. Now, being somewhat of a small-town girl, I wasn't used to this means of entering a building. Perhaps this is what caused me to have problems in doing so. At any rate, as I was trying to step into one of the wedge-shaped sections I missed my timing and my dress got caught. What a stir it created as I backed up a whole line of waiting businessmen, a few of whom came gallantly to my rescue and set the doors in reverse motion, thus extricating me from my predicament.

Needless to say this set us ninth-graders off into gales of laughter, but I had begun a calamity pattern that continued as the day wore on. Once inside the doors we thought to soothe Mr. Dunlap, who was showing growing signs of irritation, by quietly studying the many names engraved on bronze plates that covered a good portion of the wall facing the doors in the lobby.

"Looky here, Kim, here's a Gallagher. Bet there's not a Llewellyn among them." Frantically Kim searched plate after plate.

"Well, here's a Louis, and that's my grandfather's first name."

"First names don't count, sweetie." Then, "Oh, look, here's a Ryan!"

"But first names don't count, Mighty Mouse, remember?"

"Well, this is different." At that we cracked up and proceeded to find Gregory and any other name that came to mind. I even found a Scott. It was fun.

Next we boarded the elevator and were whisked to the very top, from where we looked out over the great city of New York. It was really a breathtaking view. So much to take in! We were particularly interested in seeing how many corporations in the vicinity had put signs on the top of their buildings so that Empire State Building onlookers could identify their exact location. Then we made an excursion to the gift shop and purchased some souvenirs, for the "old folks at home," and squeezed into a booth where we took pictures of each other acting goofy. Finally we emerged again onto the crowded walkways of New York City via the revolving doors. Things went a little more smoothly this time, I might add, thanks to some "help" from my friends.

The Empire State Building out of the way, we made our way on foot to a park and enjoyed a picnic lunch. The rain had stopped momentarily and the sun teased to come out. Trudy was in good spirits that day, as usual, and she was lots of fun, even if Ryan was a bit perverse at times. What made him like that? I wondered. It was while pondering this question that I stepped off the curb at the wrong time, nearly getting hit in the process. I scurried to the opposite side in an attempt to catch up with the first half of the class, who were safely across. As I neared the group my foot somehow slipped, throwing me into a full-fledged slide. In an effort to maintain my equilibrium I stabbed down with my now-folded umbrella—right into my leg—running my nylon hose very badly in the process.

In an effort to save me from myself, Trudy and Kim decided to be my personal bodyguards. They each took one of my arms and walked me the rest of the way to our next destination. I felt like a not-so-mighty mouse that day being chased by five thousand big-city pussy cats. And the more dilemmas I found myself in, the more we laughed.

We entered the subway station to catch a train that would carry us to where we would take the ferry to see Staten Island and the Statue of Liberty. The place was dimly lit, and the characters loitering along the subway walls left us with the feeling of desiring better company. We all sort of slunk together, breathing as lightly as possible of the tobacco-laden air.

When it was decided which subway train we would embark on, we walked to the proper place. There was a delay in leaving for some reason, and the fellows wandered back and forth between the train and the platform of the subway. Suddenly the signal sounded and Gregory and Edgar hopped aboard. Ryan did too, only he, being last in line, didn't quite make it, and the subway train's doors caught him about the ears. Fortunately for him he had his arms in a position to force the doors open temporarily until he could wiggle the back half of himself through. The look of surprise on his face coupled with the redness of his ears was more than we could take. Karen, Kim, and I burst with laughter, which only increased his antagonistic attitude toward us.

Once the car started, it began moving rapidly. Sitting there I scanned the faces of the car's occupants. Most of this particular group seemed harmless enough, and for a brief second I wished that we could experience another blackout such as had taken place a short time before our arrival in New York City. The excitement of it all intrigued me. How romantic! I expressed my thought to Kim and she was immediately enthusiastic.

"Wouldn't it be something?" we mused. Karen thought we were nuts. I snickered to myself as I thought what her reaction would be if she knew of my burning desire to experience the excitement of being on a sinking ship—being rescued in a lifeboat, of course.

The ferry ride was very cold and windy. We engaged ourselves in conversation with the pilot, who was rather good-looking. He supplied interesting information while we were on our way to see the Statue of Liberty. Ryan sauntered within view just as the ferry was bumping its way to a landing. He looked a

bit disturbed when he saw Kim and me chatting with the handsome pilot. The pilot took in the situation and winked at us as we left. We fairly flew off the ferry and raced to the base of the Statue of Liberty. Glancing back at the slowpokes, we darted through the doorway and began climbing with vigor. About halfway up we were struggling along with considerable effort, and for the last fifty or so steps we just dragged. Once up the stairs we peered out first one and then another of the twenty-five windows around the crown of the statue.

Getting up early and darting about here and there all day had left us a bit fatigued, and with it came more than our usual measure of foolishness. Indeed, everything we saw struck us funny one way or another. Our silliness was rippling out to the rest of the class, and they responded in kind. Trudy and Mr. Dunlap must have been glad when the day ended.

Ryan and Greg were still moody on the way back, but Kim and I managed to enjoy ourselves in spite of them. It was Kim's first trip to New York City and mine, too, except for my day at the World's Fair. We had made it a memorable one.

The events were such that we didn't want to forget them, hence a second round of epistles began.

"Dear Rat Fink . . ."

THE BIRTHDAY PARTY

WHEN we returned from our New York expedition I learned that my mother had had her own excitement. Wanting to escape from housework for a few minutes, she set out on a walk around Jason's Square. As she strolled, she had a sudden impulse to glance backward, and to her horror saw a huge steer bearing down on her. One look at him, charging with horns down, set her legs into a motion that would be considered remarkable for one of any age. Down the road she sped. Wondering how long she could keep up such a pace, she suddenly spied a farmer turning out of his barnyard onto the pavement. This good man took in the situation at a glance and promptly steered the fierce oncomer off course with his wagon and summoned his neighbor to come and round up his steer.

The remainder of mother's walk was accomplished on wobbly legs, and more than once she wondered what her fate might have been had not the farmer come along at precisely the right moment.

The week, so pleasantly broken in the middle by the class trip, passed quickly. It was Friday night. Kim and Greg had gone home with Mr. Connors, and once again I was without my companion. We had sunshine bands on Sabbath and Ryan was quite nice to me.

A dozen or so of us went to sing for some elderly people in a home. An unpleasant odor, typical of such places, assaulted our nostrils as we entered. Why did odors bother me so much? Ever since I could remember, I had been like that. The six girls in the group sang "Take Time to Be Holy," and Betty, Lisa, and I sang "My Jesus, I Love Thee." I was aware that Scott was watching me—it was a good feeling. Again I wished that he were going to our school. As Edgar played his trumpet I wondered whatever would indeed happen to me? Whom would I marry?

Would I ever have someone to call my very own? Someone who loved me all the time and would show it? I was tired of the game Ryan and I had been playing all year. And yet I knew if he did tell me he loved me, I'd be scared to death. Did he know that? What was love all about anyway?

After the musical part of the program ended, we visited with the elderly people. It must be horrible to grow old, I thought, and have nobody to care for you. Finally Dale, who had organized the group, asked Jeannie to pray, and next thing we knew we were back at the church school.

The fellowship of those young people week after week had done much to strengthen my budding belief that Christians can be happy, that God doesn't intend for us to be long-faced, and that you can have a good time while witnessing and helping others.

I had looked forward to Saturday evening all week. There was to be a birthday party for Betty at Jenkins', and a number of the young people had been invited. We all anticipated a lively time.

Maria dropped me off shortly after seven, and with a "Thanks, I'll see you later, Sis," I scurried into Jenkins' house. The place always seemed to be in an advanced state of activity, which was to be expected of a family that included five children. The youngest was still in diapers and was a real doll baby, with deep brown eyes. After a good number had arrived we made our way downstairs to the basement, where Mrs. Jenkins and Lisa and Betty and Rosie Denver were busy blowing up balloons and taking care of other last-minute details. We all mingled freely and the good time began. Ryan was his old friendly self again.

Betty and Greg were no longer dating, so Betty was "foot-loose and fancy-free" at the party that celebrated her sixteenth birthday. There were about as many boys as there were girls.

The games that had been planned were well organized and a lot of fun. Relay races involving passing Lifesavers from tooth-pick to toothpick (which everyone held in his mouth) down the line of team members created quite a stir. We also passed

oranges from neck to neck at "breakneck" speed and played musical chairs to the music of a record player.

The highlight of the evening was the game called Salt Lake City. Obviously none of the fellows had ever played it before, which only added to the fun. The boys were sent upstairs and were brought down one by one to the basement blindfolded. The idea was for them to guess which city in the United States a certain girl was thinking of, and if he could guess it within ten tries he would get a "kiss" from the girl. The "kiss" would consist of pressing his lips with a rolled-up paper towel that had been moistened and well coated with salt.

Now the city that would bring forth the "kiss" was Salt Lake City, and if the fellow wasn't getting near it by the fifth guess or so, loud whispers would begin in hopes that the blindfolded lad in the chair would pick up the clue and say "Salt Lake City" and thus receive his "reward."

Well, it worked splendidly. Every one of the fellows eventually gave the much-hoped-for answer, and we giggled with delight each time another salty "kiss" was administered. Then, of course, the boy who had just been "kissed" would watch with glee as another unknowing victim was brought as a lamb before the slaughter. If Ryan thought I'd kiss him that night he got a surprise.

There were refreshments, which included a beautifully decorated cake, and more crazy carryings on, and then it was ten-thirty. Exhausted and sweaty from all the excitement, we were ready to go home when our folks came and picked us up.

"Did you have a good time?"

"Yes," I replied as I settled down on the front seat of the car, "I surely did."

"You certainly look as if you did."

"They're a great bunch of kids."

HELLO TO THE REST OF OUR LIVES

THE closing days of school crept upon us quickly. The relief of being finished with studies for the summer was a pleasant thought indeed. No more history and no more algebra—how glorious. But overshadowing our delight was the hard fact that never would we be together in these surroundings again. I guess we were all sentimental about it, each in his or her own way. Even some of the laughter was hushed those last few days. The hallways seemed to have a sad atmosphere about them—they would experience no more whispering sessions and excited scurryings to and fro—at least from this crop of kids.

If it had been just the close of another year, things might not have seemed so final to us who were leaving; but it was the last year. Period. Next year school would begin in a new location. Never again would things be the same. The golden days of that once-in-a-lifetime year were drawing to a close. How could we make the world understand? Something as precious as this should live on and not be forgotten. This was not just any year. This year was special. The closeness and meaningful relationships had made it that way.

Standing on the step outside the back door by the typing room, Kim and I fell silent, as if trying to drink in the last memories the school year had to offer us. Tears were close.

Both of us would be selling magazines this summer, Kim in Windsor and I in Willow Run with Trudy. Greg would also be returning to Windsor, where he would work with his dad. Ryan had lined up employment with a car-wash firm and had plans of making big money. I would still see him at church.

Our relationship had changed completely. Since Fran had come, nothing had been the same. Ryan was friendly enough, and even sweet at times, but it seemed as if neither of us had been able to weather the storm that Fran had created.

It was just as well, for we were both young and in need of a lot of growing. Only God knew what events were in store for us in the years ahead and what we needed to prepare us to meet them with grace.

Yes, so much ahead of us all—both in the near future and further on down the road of life. What did it hold for us? What would this summer bring? And what would happen next year? Would God see fit to fulfill the plans that Kim and I had dreamed together?

Greg had asked me to his house near Windsor for a weekend. We would go skating on Saturday night. I was excited, honored, and *scared*. Greg wasn't the shy type that Ryan was.

Kim's interest had turned to a handsome boy in the Windsor church. He was planning to be a minister and she was pleased about that.

Standing there on the step, it seemed that life stretched out in a long rosy path from that point. We couldn't wait to start down that path. Our year in Willow Run, with its laughter and tears, was over. But, even as I looked ahead with the hopefulness of fifteen, I hated to let the past go into oblivion. Being fourteen had been such fun. It ought to be written down. That was it! Someday I would write a book about it and tell all the things that happened in Willow Run.

With one accord Kim and I stepped off the porch and walked away for the last time and into what was the beginning of a new era for both of us.